THE GRAVE AND THE GAY

Jason M. Rubin

The tale that follows
Has long been told
By fellows with flute
Fiddle or lute
And though it be old
It continues to suit
And fill the hollows

Dedication

This book is lovingly dedicated to all my friends and family who have supported me through days and nights both grave and gay. It comes too late for some, but know that I carried your faith and belief in me into these pages.

* * *

About the Author

Jason M. Rubin has been a writer all his life, a professional one since 1985 when he graduated from the University of Massachusetts, Amherst, with a degree in Journalism. He lives and works in the Boston area, where his daughters Hannah and Stella give his life deep meaning and endless joy. This is his first book.

* * *

About the Book

The Grave and the Gay is based on the 17th-century English folk ballad "Matty Groves." It is known by several variant names, including "Little Musgrave and Lady Barnard," and is classified as Child 81. In the late nineteenth century, American scholar Francis James Child collected and published 305 ballads from England and Scotland, along with their American variants. Twentieth-century recorded versions by Doc Watson (1966) and Fairport Convention (1969) are particularly recommended.

Chapter 1

Darkness. Stillness. Silence. Then cool air against skin, causing a slow rustle, a sightless reach for the goose-feather blanket. From the sudden stir Lady Barnard's eyes roll up beneath their lids. The darkness no longer is absolute. It shifts, gradually, from black to brown, from red to orange. Eventually there is light entering the room, light entering her consciousness. Now voices, muffled. But not just voices. Songs. Birds. Her eyes open. Like a bear winter denning, she arises, aroused by the siren call of appetite. For after a long, lethargic winter, the air finally felt like…

Spring! Could it be? Yes, it must!

The calendar had promised. Each day had a little warmer, a shade brighter. And now…

At long last, she realized in her still-waking mind, *spring is here!*

Convinced it was true, Lady Barnard, sprung from her bed and strode towards her window. As her face hovered near and nearly pressed against the glass, her exuberant breath created a moist fog on the interior-facing pane. Impatiently, she wiped the moisture with her hand, revealing only that the window's exterior was still wet with silver ovals of morning dew that the young day's low sun had yet to dry.

Not to be denied the sight and smell she craved, Lady Barnard thrust her small pale hands at the wooden bolts that had kept the window closed tightly against the winter chill, and struggled to work them loose. It took a few moments, for they had not been disturbed for a number of months, but at last she succeeded.

Shedding for a moment her well-schooled gentility, Lady Barnard flung open the window and into her face flew the long-awaited guest: that southwesterly wind that clipped the green fields of Dublin, carried the moist, mossy aroma of peat over the Atlantic Ocean and round the Isle of Anglesey, and at last deposited this timeworn trace of spring to the thawing English county of Lancashire, and into Lady Barnard's bedroom.

It had been a brutally hard winter – dozens in the county had died of exposure or illness – and this much-anticipated sign of change was as welcome to the weary Lancastrians as the sight of a branch in the beak of Noah's dove must have been to the survivors of the Great Deluge. Together with the increased chatter of returning birds and the reappearance of tight green buds on vines and shrubs, these heralds of the new season inspired a restless euphoria in all.

Never mind that one's breath was still clearly visible at dawn and in the evenings, or that fires as much for warmth as for cooking still burned in people's hearths. No, impatience prevailed and folks were already out and about, preparing for the Eastertime celebrations to come.

Mind you, in spring impatience is indeed a virtue. It is the impatience of the crocus pushing through the damp, softening soil that calls nature again to life. It is the impatience of the sun, no longer intent to give way to darkness so soon after supper, that gives light and thus encouragement to all human and natural pursuits. And it is the impatience of time itself that stands not a day longer in a single season than it must, because tomorrow is never inevitable and each day, each season, is a gift to the earth and all who live upon it.

That the advent of spring and the festival of Easter coincided was Divine inspiration, so it seemed to Lady Barnard. For the very stakes that her father used to support his nascent tomatoes and peas in spring reminded her of the cross in her church upon which the wooden sculpture of Jesus was nailed, awaiting his own ripening in heaven. Even the Lord's nickname, the Lamb of God, reminded her of the fresh lamb that her father killed and her mother cooked and that graced their festival table on Easter afternoon.

In this season rich with tradition, small bands of enterprising young men gathered in taverns, on porches, in fields, and even in the rear pews on Sunday mornings, enlisting like-minded merry-makers to join their pace-egging troupes. "Pace", of course, is from the Latin *pacha*, or spring. And eggs are the season's most common symbol of rebirth. In this part of the country, the pace-eggers journey from town to town each Easter Sunday in wild costumes and with a song of entreaty, requesting favors – usually eggs boiled in onionskin or coins of any value – which they repay with a farcical play.

The *dramatis personae* of this play includes such rich characters as the Lady Gay, the Soldier Brave, and the notorious Old Tosspot, whose coal-blackened face gapes and guffaws above the basket he waves to hold the aforementioned favors. In his other hand, the stronger one in fact, he holds a straw tail stuffed with pins, which he swings madly towards those who either are slow in paying into the basket or who have the temerity to try and steal its precious contents.

Following the play – not the Passion narrative as such, although a comical death and a magical rebirth of sorts usually transpires – Old Tosspot again bullies the crowd for favors. When the audience disperses for their own feasts, the eggs are eaten (and shells crushed, lest witches use them as boats to spread their spells and unholy mischief to other locales, so the legend goes) and the coins shared and pocketed, or else tendered in exchange for mugs of ale. The pace-eggers then make their way to another village and the entire act plays out again. By the end of the holiday, the pace-eggers would have consumed enough eggs and ale to keep them in their beds well into the following day.

Yet even as the men were organizing their bands; even as the women were cleaning their houses and making room in their kitchens for the game they would pluck and cook, and the pies and cakes they would bake; even as children dreaded the clean, newly knit clothes they had to wear to church, and the switch they knew would be taken to them if they misbehaved during the service, even with all this activity, this anticipation, at high pitch – still Easter was half a fortnight away.

Perhaps a milder winter would not have inspired such relentless desire of spring and all its vernal wonders.

Yet rarely is spring met with indifference, especially here in Lancashire, still a Catholic stronghold, where the faithful greet this time of year with hope, for all have the capacity to change, to grow. And if the sun finds us and we strengthen in the warmth of its light, we, too, may be reborn in an eternal spring, a perfected flower in God's vast, loving garden.

It was in this happy and hopeful atmosphere that Lady Barnard drew the fresh peaty air deeply into her nostrils, and in exhaling released a winter's worth of loneliness and frustration. The crisp, invigorating breeze felt good on her alabaster face, framed as ever by dark straight hair she drew tightly at the back in a bun. As she had just arisen, it now fell randomly about her shoulders with a few black strands strewn across her face. She closed her eyes, savoring the moment, and then opened them to see which persons were out in the crisp, clean air.

What Lady Barnard saw first were the few servants her husband employed out in the yard going about their morning chores. She also saw townspeople passing her grand home on the winding dirt road. By all accounts, a typical morning sight. But today, instead of white, the endless, hopeless white of cold and imposing snow, there were colorful figures in motion against a deepening green and brown background. Faces were uncovered, revealing pleasant-looking people with things to do and the will to do them – not bundled creatures too cold to socialize, rushing from one hearth to another.

I bid you welcome, spring, she thought to herself, *and may winter not soon return.*

In truth, as cold as it had been out of doors the past few months, it had been just as frigid within her stately home – and for an even longer duration. Though she was not a prisoner in her house, her comings and goings were carefully controlled by Lord Barnard, who had an odd yet intensely adamant dislike of people gossiping about what went on in each other's lives and homes. Concerned that Lady Barnard would reveal personal information about their lives, he stringently limited her trips into town and never let her go alone; though in truth, it likely was not so much what *did* go on at home that fueled his fears, but rather what did *not*.

After ten years of marriage, there had been no children. Furthermore, it had been far too long, in Lady Barnard's opinion, since the act of conception had even been attempted. Now, with the coming of spring, Lord Barnard would resume his hunting trips. She would be left alone, which, while not ideal, she found preferable to being ignored.

This day, however, as nature's insistent cycle moved one-quarter turn, as other people's lives were opening up like laurel buds, Lady Barnard wanted no longer to be so constrained, as if she were a mourning dove in too cramped a cage. She desired to meet people, speak with them, and revel in the attention of the ladies who would envy her fine clothing; perhaps read in a young man's eyes that there was more to her appeal than that overly familiar visage that appeared in her looking glass.

Then a scowl formed on her face, as she turned away from the window. Lady Barnard knew she could never be like the young girls out there on the street, fluttering about and flirting in plain view, with no care nor shame. Raised with no special privileges in terms of money or station, she was the fairest of three daughters born to a small farmer and his oft-sickly wife. Despite their circumstances, it was her father's intention that she be well-married. As such, he traded sacks of cornmeal he had milled himself for lessons in etiquette and domestic skills for his daughter, that she would be a draw not only for her looks but also for her suitability in any sort of company.

She was taught to be polite, demure, submissive yet capable. She ably learned literature, geography, and mathematics yet was instructed not to volunteer opinions on these matters. It was better to possess knowledge than to demonstrate it, her teacher told her. Of these subjects, she was particularly enamored of the first two for they promised vistas beyond her reach, adventures that seemed otherworldly, and stories of courage and daring such as she could only imagine being close to.

When the match was made with Lord Barnard, she did as she had been prepared to do. She held herself with a dignity free from pomposity and a wisdom expressed in whispers of competence as a given situation required. Yet as Lord Barnard's constraints upon her grew more numerous, frequent, and intrusive, her only response was to become more silent, withdrawn, and resigned. Thus it was that Lady Barnard sadly turned back to the window, continuing to spy enviously on those who have fewer means yet far more freedom than she.

It may not be a good life they lead, she thought, *but it is a life they own, a life they control. I am no more in charge of my destiny than these French draperies are of theirs. In truth,* she admitted, *I am much like the draperies, the furniture, the china and silver. We all are affectations, mere decorations for my Lord.*

We are that, she thought, *all that, yet nothing more.*

Distressed again, as if spring were still just a distant dream, her focus became distracted. Though she continued to look out the window into the yard below, in truth she saw nothing; or rather, her mind did not acknowledge what was there within her view. Thus it was that she took no notice of the tall figure passing into the scope of her vision, the handsome man named by his long-deceased mother Matthew Musgrave.

To his friends and lovers, and he had many of both, he was Matty. Sporting fair features and a confident gait, Matty was Lord Barnard's stable hand, and had Lady Barnard truly seen him she would have thought him familiar-looking yet been unable to identify neither his name nor his role. The stable was but one of many places to which she never ventured – though in this case, it was of her own choosing that she avoided it.

Matty, however, looked towards the grand home as he crossed the yard and could see Lady Barnard's eyes facing his direction. He assumed she was looking at him, but as she did not appear about to give an order, he continued on his way.

Fewer than twenty paces hence, Matty came upon Alexandra McLean doing the Barnards' laundry under the calm March sky. A red handkerchief held back her long, straw-colored, slightly curly mane. Beautiful even in damp, loose-fitting work clothes, she stood chest-high to her visitor. As Matty approached, she gladly suspended her work and placed a lid on the tall cast iron cauldron of water that sat on an open wood fire beside her.

"Good morning, Alexandra," said Matty, with a knowing grin on his strong and pleasant face.

"And to you, Matty," Alexandra replied, dabbing her moist forehead with her apron.

"Will I see you in the loft tonight, fair maiden?" he inquired.

With mock incredulity, she said, "Oh, is it my turn again so soon, then?"

"Whatever could you mean?" came another mock-incredulous reply, met with a bemused smile and a few shakes of Alexandra's fair head as she returned to her waiting work pile.

"I shan't promise you," she replied, not looking up. "I don't see myself finishing before supper, unless I collapse where I stand. The Lady instructed me to wash all the quilts today, though I'll never get to hers if she doesn't wake up already."

"Odd thing, she was just staring at me from her window as I passed along from the stable."

"It's not so strange for a woman to stare at *you*, now, is it, Matty?"

"Well, she's not just any woman, is she? And I doubt she even knows my name."

"Ah, but I'm sure she knows a pretty face. And I believe she has been lonely for a man's attentions," Alexandra added.

"What makes you say that?

"I wash the bed linens," she whispered, raising her eyes from the steaming cauldron to her handsome caller. "Many a tale is told in soiled sheets. The Lord's and the Lady's are unusually clean, if you understand my meaning."

"Perhaps they employ that long dining table in place of a bed," said Matty.

"I would prefer hard wood or even cold marble to the straw you sleep on."

"Then accept this offer. Tonight you will ride me like a horseman and I will take the quills in my backside."

"You are a true gentleman, Matty. A true –"

At that moment, the occasional lovers were interrupted by Darnell, the Barnards' personal assistant. As a "house" servant, he boasted a more prestigious position than those like Matty and Alexandra, who toiled out of doors or in other quarters. Darnell even had a room of his own in the Barnards' basement, with a door for his ingress and egress so that he could enter and exit his room without having to go through the house proper.

"Matty Musgrave," Darnell called.

"I am here," replied Matty.

"Lord Barnard wishes to see you immediately."

"For what purpose?"

"I neither wish to know nor need to know," Darnell replied, without the disinterest he would wish to display. "It is my Lord's desire to speak with you and while I do not comprehend the affection he seems to have for you lately, I am merely fulfilling my duty in informing you of his urgent request."

Looking down at Matty's feet, Darnell added, "Might I suggest you change your shoes so as not to track manure into the home?"

"Lord Barnard loves his horses and he loves me," teased Matty. "How, then, can he be upset if my shoes bring both his loves to him?"

As Darnell stifled a shout and Alexandra muffled a laugh, Matty bid them good day. When the strutting stable hand neared the house, Darnell said to Alexandra, "He is a disgusting brute."

"Yes, though you have to admit he is honest about it," she replied.

"You're too good for him, you know."

"So you've told me. Thank you for your concern, Darnell. Now if you don't mind, I need to attend to the washing."

"I can do better by you."

"Can you, then? How? You work *in* the house, but you are not *master* of it."

"Alexandra, you know I have feelings for you. I am a decent man. I have a good position. The Lord and Lady treat me well. As my wife, you would improve your standing with them."

"Is that your offer, then?" she asked with a faint smile. "That I should be a servant's wife? Am I to be servant to a servant?"

"Well, what can Matty offer you?" Darnell demanded to know.

"Laughter, Darnell. Laughter and passion. And nothing more because I desire nothing more. You know

Matty. He'll not be chained to a wife, nor I to a husband. It's enough for me that I can sit out on a spring morning and earn a wage and a meal."

"You're a lovely girl, Alexandra. But you have no sense. I will not stop courting you, not until I have proven to you that I would be a better husband for you than that, that...stable hand."

"That 'stable hand' may not be cultured, Darnell, he may be nothing more than a raggle taggle gypsy, but he knows what he is, he's not ashamed, and he doesn't put on airs. You're a decent man, true, but you're not your own man, are you? You're the man the Barnards demand you be. That's the difference between you and Matty. You try so hard to please that it's impossible to distinguish between your position and your person. That's why even though I've known you longer than I've known Matty, I've no clue as to your soul. Yes, you show interest in me, but you've never shown passion."

Just then a bell rang, its bird-like warble emanating from the open window above.

"That's Lady Barnard," said Darnell. "I must go to her. Remember what I have said, Alexandra. I don't know how I will prove my love and my worth to you. But I will. I swear it upon all that is right and holy."

And with that, Darnell followed the same steps that Matty took into the house, looking down all the way to check for traces of manure. Alexandra watched wordlessly as he walked away, then returned her attention to the piles of laundry that had not lessened during her conversations.

She placed another log on the neglected fire down below and submerged a feather-stuffed comforter in the hot, soapy water, stirring it with a large wooden paddle as she thought on the disparate propositions Darnell and Matty had made to her.

Chapter 2

The Barnards' residence sat on a large parcel of land, equidistant to the ocean due east and the Forest of Bowland to the west. With the house situated close to the road in front, the bulk of the property was in the rear, out of the public's view. As such, the village square to which Lady Barnard longed to go was a short southward walk – made longer by her husband's obstinacy.

Though not a master horseman by any means, Lord Barnard enjoyed taking morning rides by himself. Typically, he would circle the edges of his property, never getting too close to either the ocean (for he could not swim) nor the village (for he was not a sociable man). He hunted in the forest in every season except summer (too much heat, too many insects) and winter (too frigid, not enough game), but was a poor navigator and thus often had to hire a guide.

The impressive house, built by Lord Barnard's father and uncles when Lord Barnard was but a bump in his mother's belly, was large; no other home in the village had near as much living space. Strange, then, that so little of it was actually lived in. The Barnards were not wont to entertain and so rarely hosted parties. Business associates and relatives would come for dinner occasionally but on most days the house would hold the bare minimum of Lord and Lady Barnard, plus a few servants coming and going as necessary.

The couple employed just five servants, though two of them – a cook and a house cleaner, chatty people both – had recently been dismissed by Lord Barnard. The others, of course, were Darnell, who coordinated the maintenance and operations of the home and its occupants; Alexandra, the laundress; and Matty, who minded the horses. In the absence of both cook and cleaner, Alexandra had been asked to mop the floors and dust the draperies in addition to her usual duties.

Their meals in the interim were simple, prepared either by Lady Barnard or Darnell. It was beneath their means, yet neither Lord nor Lady Barnard was eager to replace the fired servants, preferring the increased quiet and privacy. (This was, after all, the house in which Lord Barnard had been raised, and he was disinclined to change it much, or to drive any more foot traffic into it than was necessary. At any rate, for most minor chores he would rather fend for himself than invite and involve additional persons into his surroundings.)

Such traffic, as Matty did now, generally entered by way of the wide front porch. With a waist-high wall in front and no chairs set out on the floor, the porch seemed more a buffer against the outside world than an entrée to the home. The unadorned front door opened to a great room that connected to a hallway on the left, with three rooms and a staircase accessible to the right. Directly to the rear were a plush, hunter's green sofa and four matching chairs with arms. Just to the side of them was an ornate spinet harpsichord purchased in Italy that was hand-painted and signed by its maker, the master craftsman Girolamo Zenti.

As Matty entered the great room he passed beneath a large round chandelier fashioned by Lord Barnard's father from a wagon wheel; the fine workmanship notwithstanding, the rustic piece contrasted with the elegance of the room's furnishing. Centered underneath it was a square crimson carpet spotted here and there with blobs of candle wax that had dripped from above. Matty's carefree steps pressed the wax deeper into the carpet's otherwise well-cared-for threads.

The hallway to the left led to two vacant rooms formerly occupied by the cook and house cleaner. (Aside from Darnell's quarters in the basement, no other servants had rooms in the house. Matty lived in a room outfitted with a wood stove and a makeshift slop sink – really just a half barrel set above a hole in the ground – attached to the rear of the stable, the comfort of which often depended on the direction of the wind. Alexandra was allowed a bed when needed in her cousin Andrew's home in the village. She hoped to be invited to occupy one of the empty rooms in the house, though such invitation had yet to be tendered.)

The rooms to the right were the kitchen, accessible through a door at the far left end of the wall, and a dining room and study that were essentially partitioned areas of the great room itself as opposed to discretely constructed spaces. With so few inhabitants and visitors, additional walls and doors were deemed superfluous.

The staircase to which Matty approached, also crimson carpeted with a railing painted white, led to a perpendicular hallway sitting atop the dining room and study. Once at the top of the stairs, to the left was Lord Barnard's bedroom; to the right was Lady Barnard's. From the start of their marriage, Lord Barnard had insisted on separate quarters. His he used for both sleep and study. Fastidious about its order and cleanliness, Lord Barnard further insisted that their sexual activities, such as they were, be confined to his wife's bed and bedroom.

As Matty ascended the staircase, a wooden sword rack rose to his view. Built by Lord Barnard's father, it hung in the center of the upstairs hallway. The cherry wood the elder Barnard used gave it the appearance of having been glazed long ago with actual blood, since dried and darkened. The four rungs held two pairs of swords: one pair, worn and dull, was originally owned – and apparently often used – by the senior Barnard; the other pair was purchased two summers prior by Lord Barnard when on business in Versailles. There he'd taken fencing lessons, though these swords, ornate and expensive, were for display only, and their silvery glint beckoned imposingly to Matty as he approached Lord Barnard's study.

Matty had been tending the horses for more than a year now; this was his second spring wielding brush and shovel in the stable. He had not come recommended to Lord Barnard, nor had Lord Barnard issued any broadside advertising such a position. After all, before Matty arrived he owned but two horses that he had cared for himself.

It was early in March of the previous year when Thomas Erickson, a printer, had to sell off some of his possessions in order to avoid jail for nearly killing a young man named Henry Harrison, whom he believed had disgraced his eldest daughter. The weapon had been the steel poker with which the widower was tending his fire.

Despite the seemingly improvised choice of instrument, this was not a crime of passion but rather one very much planned and premeditated. The precipitating incident had occurred four days earlier, but Erickson had heard of it only the day before, and not from his daughter (who denied it) but from the man he'd hired to muck out his stable daily and perform a complete cleaning every Sabbath morning: one Matthew Musgrave.

The talk in the local tavern was that Matty and Henry had a disagreement between themselves, perhaps over Erickson's daughter, a common point of interest for the two men. Regardless of how and for what reason the accusation came to be made, Erickson invited Henry to his home one night under the ruse that he was eager to give a potential suitor his blessing. Once the poor lad crossed the threshold, however, Erickson came at him with the poker, and only his daughter's impassioned screams for mercy saved the young man's life.

Neighbors, alarmed by the girl's wailing, soon rushed in. One seized Erickson from behind, wrapping his arm around the deranged man's neck, while the other took hold of the weapon, now crimson-flecked. Henry, on the floor and barely conscious, was given a blanket and consoled. A large gash on his temple soaked through several cloths before a doctor could arrive with thread to close the wound.

Erickson, being a man of some stature in the business community, was held in a locked room overnight, chiefly to let his fury subside, but otherwise was allowed to remain free. However, he was ordered to pay restitution to Henry's parents (the boy being too young to collect the fine himself and in no condition at the time to make use of it) and so auctioned off his two horses to raise the money.

Lord Barnard attended the auction, though more out of curiosity to see the final act of a local tragedy than to acquire Erickson's mares. Yet Matty, who was also present and for much the same reason as Lord Barnard, saw an opportunity for advancement and, perhaps, immunity, and so approached him with a proposition.

"Lord Barnard," spoke Matty with head bowed, "I beg your forgiveness but may I have a word with you? I am Matty Musgrave, Mr. Erickson's stable hand, and I know these horses well. They are fine animals indeed. I have seen your stable in passing and it is large enough to provide shelter for these two. Furthermore, the addition of these creatures would make you the largest horse owner in the village, which is fitting for such an important man as yourself."

That Lord Barnard was accustomed to flattery did not render Matty's brief soliloquy, made with such a sweet mouth on a handsome face, any the less effective. Barely concealing a smile, Lord Barnard replied, "And an important man such as I has the time to care for four horses? How would I manage the doubling of my stable?"

"Well, sir, prior to this unfortunate incident Mr. Erickson was most pleased with my work," said Matty. "After today, the horses will be gone and my skills will be unneeded here. Should you choose to purchase Mr. Erickson's horses, it would be my honor to transfer my services to you, to care not only for these animals, but for your other two as well."

"Very well, then," said Lord Barnard. "I will pay you what Erickson paid you for one month. If I am satisfied with you, I will pay you one-and-a-half times your current salary. This assumes, of course, that I make the winning bid. If not, you have no job with me."

"If you don't mind my saying so, sir, as I look at the crowd assembled here today, I see not another man whose purse is as deep as yours, nor one whose honor and generosity are a match for yours," Matty said with an exaggeratedly reverent bow.

As it turned out, Lord Barnard did purchase the horses and gained Matty's services as well. After a month, Lord Barnard, as promised, raised Matty's wages. That summer, during which he spent considerably more time observing Matty's work (tiring work as it was in the summer heat, Matty often soaked through his shirt and removed it), Lord Barnard raised his wages again, now paying him double what Erickson had.

In the fall, Lord Barnard was away often, hunting and attending to business in other towns and villages. He returned two weeks before the solstice and every week or so after that would summon Matty to his office. He had no particular request or order to give to his charismatic stable hand. Rather, these meetings were a process by which Lord Barnard got to know Matty better. Occasionally, he would give Matty a gift, either a small trinket he picked up while on business or else an extra ration of food. Unbeknownst to him, Matty often gave both types of gifts to Alexandra.

Matty, accustomed to seizing onto advantages, did not question the Lord's generosity or interest in him. He attributed it to the quality of his work; and indeed, the horses were well cared for and the stable fairly immaculate.

At the same time, he was careful not to give his benefactor reason to question his continuing employment and so judiciously engaged in half-truths and omissions when Lord Barnard asked about his background. What wasn't expressed, Matty reasoned, needn't be explained.

As Matty reached the door of Lord Barnard's quarters, he thought to look down and back, just to see if he indeed had tracked any detritus into the house. Not seeing evidence of such, he turned back to the door and knocked two raps.

"Enter," came the voice from inside. Matty opened the door and stepped in. Lord Barnard rose from his writing table and greeted Matty warmly, placing his left hand over Matty's right, which was in the clasp of Lord Barnard's writing hand. "It is nice to see you again, Matty," said Lord Barnard. "How are the horses this morning?"

"Eager to be ridden, sir, in this accommodating air," Matty answered.

"It is a lovely day now, isn't it?" Lord Barnard released Matty's hand and took a few steps past him to close the door. "Come sit here, my boy." Matty took hold of the chair next to Lord Barnard's writing desk and sat down.

"Matty, you have served me very well over the past year. I am most pleased with your work."

Matty hastened to interject his appreciation for the comment, but Lord Barnard stopped him with a raised hand. Matty's gaze fixed upon Lord Barnard's open palm, which faced him, and he noticed how much cleaner it was than his, how much smoother, without the calluses that the handles and shafts of shovels and pitchforks caused. *What things do these untroubled hands touch and caress,* he thought. *If I had such hands with which to touch Alexandra, how much more pleased would she be?*

"Please just listen, Matty," Lord Barnard continued. "In the year that I've known you, I've become quite fond of you. I think you know that." Despite the last statement, Lord Barnard arched his eyebrows in a silent query, which Matty acknowledged and affirmed – also silently – with a quick nod of his head.

"I must divulge some rather personal information to you. What I am about to say to you is very important and I want you to hear it. But I must ask you to remain silent about it. You must not utter a word about this matter to anyone. Do you understand?"

Again, a silent nod of assent.

"Matty, Lady Barnard and I didn't know each other when we married. As is the custom, our respective fathers made the match. But I accepted it because I respected my father and also was ready to build a life for myself. Every professional man needs a wife to manage his home and accommodate his...needs. So I married Lady Barnard and thus made a commitment to her. Now, when one undertakes such a commitment, one has certain hopes and ideals. Marriage, to me, was a way of enhancing my station, enjoying companionship of course, but also providing offspring. I suppose every man desires a son, an heir to his estate, someone whom he could look in the eyes and see a younger reflection of himself. Someone to impart his beliefs and values to, someone who would look up to him and be loyal to him. Who would be a friend to his father and share a special bond. Do you understand?"

Matty nodded, though such a relationship between a father and a son was foreign to him.

"Matty, I'm sorry, this is difficult to say, particularly to one in my employ. And that is why it is so essential that you not share what I am about to say to anyone. Matty, my marriage to Lady Barnard has not...fulfilled me quite as I had hoped it would. After ten years of marriage, I have no children, and no –. Well, it is enough to say that I choose to wait no longer.

"Matty, I need to know that my possessions and my affairs will be maintained by someone whom I trust, someone whom I love. And I do love you, Matty, as I would my own son. Of course, I cannot leave my estate to a stable boy. And so I would like to make you into a gentleman, an educated man. There is much I can teach you, much that I want you to know, the proper dress, manners, knowledge of politics, business, history, and national affairs. I want to take you from the stable and make you presentable to people and institutions of great prestige. I want to make you worthy of being my heir, Matty. Do you understand? You will essentially be my son. In fact, legally you will be my next of kin. Do you understand what I am offering you?"

"I believe I do, sir…yet I don't know how to respond," said Matty, and this was as true a statement as any he had ever uttered in this room. "This is unlike anything I have ever heard to happen. What am I to do?"

"It is up to me to make this happen, Matty," said Lord Barnard. "First, I must confer with my solicitor. Then I must hire a new stable boy. Lastly, I will commence to teach you in the ways of sophisticated men."

Matty sat, stunned, as if he'd just been told of a dear personal loss, yet he was, in fact, being offered something of great value. Perhaps it was more the feeling of being given a fine coat made in some exotic land, like China, yet it is tailored to fit a man of much smaller or larger dimensions. A gift, then, that is precious yet not practical; or one that must be appreciated even if it is not desired. Regardless, it was not a gift that Matty could easily refuse. In the whirl of his mind he thought of how he would benefit from Lord Barnard's largesse. Yet still he could not seem to register an emotion approximating gratitude.

Lord Barnard disturbed his silent reflections. "I can see you have grasped the enormity of my offer," he said. "I do not expect you to be entirely comfortable with the idea of adopting a new life to replace your old one, limited though it is – at least not right away. But you will have time to think on it. I want you to make sure the horses are ready for a hunting trip. I plan to leave three days hence and I will be gone past Easter. Darnell has all the details, yet I have not told him nor anyone else – not even Lady Barnard – that which I have revealed to you this morning. You have been uncharacteristically quiet these last few minutes. Remain that way about this matter, or else there may be severe consequences for both of us. Do you understand?"

"I do, sir," said Matty, now finding his voice again. "And I appreciate your…affection for me. May I leave now to tend to your horses?"

"Of course, Matty. Thank you." As Matty turned to leave, Lord Barnard added, "I wish I could take you with me on this trip. But there will be many opportunities for us to spend time together in the future."

"Yes, sir," replied Matty, still facing the door, which now he hurriedly walked through and down the steps, passing Darnell, who was answering the Lady's bell. Darnell looked down and behind, checking as Matty had done earlier to see if flakes of manure and pieces of straw had dropped from the stable hand's boots. Almost annoyed to find the carpet clean, Darnell continued to climb the stairs. As he neared the top, he saw Lord Barnard's door close, though he did not see Lord Barnard. It was as if a spectre or a sharp wind had done the job.

Darnell turned then to the right, past the sword display, and went down the hall to the room at the end, the private quarters of Lady Barnard.

Chapter 3

As aide to both Lord and Lady Barnard, Darnell had seen and heard many things that the people of the village would wish to have known. Yet he understood that to be a good house servant, one must be discreet. And Darnell always wanted to be known as a man with whom one can entrust a secret. Even when Lord or Lady Barnard asked him about the other, he was very careful to give an appropriately vague reply. For even if, say, Lady Barnard wanted to know what her husband had been discussing with a certain visitor, it would not do to admit that he had been listening to the conversation.

In order to be confident that their own privacy would be protected, both the Barnards had to believe that Darnell had little to share about the other. Darnell cultivated that belief through his own admirable restraint.

And indeed there were things he had heard and witnessed that would give a gossiper many hours' worth of salacious details with which to command and satisfy an audience. For example, Darnell was witness to the fact that Lord Barnard had something of a temper, was fastidious about his personal space and papers, and was not entirely comfortable in the company of women. For her part, Lady

Barnard could be moody and withdrawn, had a taste for wine at all hours of the day, and spent more of her husband's money on items of fancy than he was aware of – or would likely approve.

Though Darnell knew all these things (and more), to his credit in four years of service he had never spoken of them. Unlike Matty, Darnell did come recommended, though some deception was involved. A visiting Lord Sanders paid a call on Lord Barnard, bearing a note of introduction from a mutual acquaintance who was an advisor to the governor. Lord Sanders had brought Darnell with him, with the story that the boy's parents had been in his employ for many years, and he had promised them that when Darnell turned 18 years of age Lord Sanders would arrange honorable employment for him. Lord Sanders had educated Darnell himself and the boy could be trusted to be loyal, prompt, and courteous.

This last sentence was true; the rest of his story was not. In fact, Darnell was Lord Sanders' son, although the mother was the cook in the Sanders household. Sadly, she died shortly after giving birth to him. Lord Sanders convinced Lady Sanders that they should raise the poor orphan themselves. Not knowing the identity of the father, Lady Sanders agreed. The boy grew up privileged and educated. When he turned 18, however, the housekeeper, an elderly woman who had taken sick and did not expect to live much longer, told Darnell the truth about his origins. Shocked, he confronted his father. This caused quite a row, and Lord Sanders decided it was time to grant the boy his independence. He secured his son's silence by threatening to harm Lady Sanders, who had raised Darnell with all the caring and love a woman can give to a child.

And so, Darnell willingly let himself be bought by Lord Barnard. Since that time, he became known for being a very capable worker, though unquestionably humorless and stern. In truth, he had long decided that he would exact revenge on his father for his deception and cruelty, all the while mourning for the mother he never knew. Lord and Lady Barnard were none the wiser about Darnell's background, yet it had left him with qualities they much appreciated in his role as their personal assistant.

Though he would never admit it to anyone, in his heart Darnell favored Lady Barnard greatly over her husband. For no good reason, simply on the basis of gender, he had projected Lord Sanders onto Lord Barnard and his deceased mother onto Lady Barnard. Which is not to say that he loved her, certainly not with the love of a boy to his mother or that of a man to his wife. Yet he did pity her. And as that pity did soften his heart, a certain attraction for her had but recently asserted itself within him. It was based largely on a sense that he should save her, as he could never have saved his own mother. He was, therefore, somewhat protective of her and often struggled to show Lord Barnard the honor and respect he was due without betraying his true feelings, either in the tone of his voice or the expression on his face.

All this, of course, is merely to give the reader an understanding of what is to transpire next. Darnell had not been waiting on this explanation. He already had knocked and had entered Lady Barnard's private quarters. She had handed Darnell a list of items for him to purchase for her in the village. He would have to go to the seamstress, to the market, and to Mr. McDougall, the old Scot who arranges flowers for the church, who had promised to make her a fine bonnet for Easter. Darnell agreed and asked Lady Barnard if there was anything else she wished of him.

"No, not really, Darnell," she replied.

"Then I shall attend to these tasks straight away."

"No," she said, a bit too quickly, perhaps. A bit too forcefully. "No, please, if you don't mind, I…I wish you to stay and chat for a few minutes."

"As you desire, my Lady," said Darnell, feeling rather pleased.

"I'm sorry, Darnell, but it has been a long winter, hasn't it? One gets rather lonely during the winter, one stays indoors. Of course, I'm not one to take rides or walk through the village. Lord Barnard wishes me to stay close to home usually, as you well know. But lately I feel I've been rather trapped, as if in a prison or something. Not just lately in fact, for a long time, a very long time now. And… well, spring is here and I've got it into my head that I don't wish to be quite so alone anymore."

"Yes, I see," Darnell lied, hoping she would elucidate further.

"I think this spring I should like to go out more from time to time," she continued. "To the village, I mean. Obviously, I will go to church on Easter Sunday, which is soon, but I don't wish to go out only then."

After a brief pause she continued softly, almost timidly, "What…do you think of that idea, Darnell?"

Darnell replied, "I should think it would be good for your constitution to be out in the fresh air, my Lady. I imagine as well that it would give the villagers a great deal of pleasure to see you more frequently."

Lady Barnard was pleased with this response. "Do you really think so?"

"I do indeed, my Lady," said Darnell, lying again though with the most noble of intentions. "Please forgive my saying so, but without your presence the village itself is like a flower that has no scent or a bird with no song."

Darnell thought he saw Lady Barnard blush. It was not readily apparent because she looked down shyly upon hearing his words, kinder words than any she had heard before in her marriage. "That is very gracious of you to say, Darnell." Then the Lady summoned the courage to raise her head and look directly at Darnell, even taking a step towards him, so that they were but three paces apart.

"Darnell, I know I can trust you with this," she said. "Lord Barnard does not…visit me very often anymore. You know what I mean. At night. He is a very busy man. But I have wondered recently if I am…still…attractive. Of course, you are a young man and your eyes are drawn to lovely young girls, as well they should. But until now, I didn't know whether someone would ever again consider me desirable.

"Tell me," she continued after a short pause, "is it true that Lord Barnard is going off on a hunting trip over the Easter holiday?"

Sensing that this was not private information, he replied truthfully. "Yes, my Lady. Lord Barnard will be leaving with a small party three days hence and is not expected to return until after the holiday."

"In that case," said Lady Barnard, "I should like to ask if you would accompany me to church on Easter Sunday as my escort."

Now it was his turn to blush. "It would be my honor, my Lady."

Darnell would have said more, but his well-trained ears noticed that Lord Barnard was approaching. Indeed, he came swiftly through the door without knocking or announcing himself, startling Lady Barnard.

"Darnell, would you excuse us, please?" he asked. "Of course, my Lord," Darnell replied. Turning to Lady Barnard, he bowed, said "My Lady," and left the room, closing the door behind him. He stayed near to the door for a few seconds, then walked down the hall and turned left to descend the stairs. His heart was racing with an excitement that he rarely had cause to feel. He was glad to be sent into town, for he feared he could not yet conceal his racing emotions. A walk in the brisk spring air would be just right.

As he set off on his errands, Darnell quietly cursed his own lauded trait of discretion.

Chapter 4

It was not difficult to understand Matty's appeal to women, nor his success with them. Standing half a head above average height, he appeared strong and solid, yet not intimidating. His thick raven hair hung nearly level with his pronounced collarbone, though he took better care of the equine manes he brushed every day than of his own tousled locks. His eyes were dark as well, though lit from inside by an impish joy that contradicted one's first impression of them: that they beheld a deep melancholy.

His skin was a shade darker than that of his fellow villagers, and there was talk that he had Spanish blood, though his nose and profile suggested an Italian or perhaps even a Turk. His full, salmon-colored lips seemed ever to be smiling and his smile was broad and true. His hands and limbs were firm. Though he had worked with horses for a number of years, he himself was not a skilled rider. He came to his livelihood because he needed one, and because most ladies were very fond of horses.

Matty had an extraordinary appetite for women and he rarely went unsated for long. Yet any strong appetite is driven by a significant hunger, and hunger is a form of emptiness. So it was with Matty that for all the good fortune that fell upon his exterior, inside he tended a private void that he would permit no other person to see or to know or inquire about.

Born in the dark heart of winter to poor, hardworking parents – his father a cobbler, his mother a mender – Matty was one from a set of twins. His brother emerged first, stillborn. So great was his parents' grief that until his mother felt a new strike of physical pain that nearly matched her emotional agony, it was little noticed that he was coming not far behind. Matty's first human experience, then, was an encompassing sadness.

He was raised with care and tenderness by his parents, but the sense of loss in their lives was palpable. When they looked at him, they saw the empty space next to him as well. As a child, Matty was unaware that he had shared his mother's womb with a brother he would never know outside of it. He came to believe, therefore, that he was born incomplete, as if there were an organ or limb present in other children that was absent in him. He feared his deformity would cause him to be taken away like others he had heard about who had been cursed in the womb by witches or because of their mothers' sins.

When, as a ten-year-old, he was finally told the story of his birth, he at first was relieved to know that the problem was neither with him nor caused by him. Yet as he grew and matured, he understood that his parents had been in pain all his life. He began then to feel jealousy towards his dead brother. Never named, the blue baby would remain innocent forever, while Matty, who indulged in the merry mischief of all healthy boys, would occasionally receive the rod, the hand, or a sharp verbal rebuke.

And then, as a teenaged young man, his perspective shifted again. Seeking to know himself, it pained him to realize he would never know his brother. This sibling he had either despised or been ignorant of would have been his mirror image. Matty would have been able to observe and understand himself by watching his brother. In turn, his brother would be uniquely capable of understanding and supporting him. Matty's closest friend would never be known to him.

From that time to the present, Matty felt nearly the same sting as his parents had felt. Yet while they had been consumed by their misery, Matty vowed to avenge it. He would live, live well, and live for both his brother and for himself. He would not face the world with bitterness or despair. Rather, he would express the affection that he and his parents had not had the opportunity to bestow on his brother, and the simple satisfaction in being that his parents were unable to show to him (for he was a living and constant reminder of their tragedy).

Of course, it helped no small amount that Matty possessed both the physical assets and the force of personality that made fulfilling his goals no difficult task.

At age sixteen, his parents died of heartbreak – or perhaps they simply lost the will to go on living. Mere weeks apart from each other, his father and then his mother took sick and expired quickly. Matty left his parents' home to embark on a life that only he could provide himself. He took on any task for which he could earn even a pittance. When a slightly demented widow hired him to repair a hole in one of her dining room walls, she paid him in flesh in advance and offered him room and board until the work was done. One would have thought that hole had been enormous, for a fortnight passed before he emerged from the house. And in looking back, one would not doubt that the dining room had been less fully transformed than he.

Word spread about "Little Musgrave" and his willingness and ability to please, and he was kept busy by maiden and matron alike, all the while refining his art while fulfilling his vow. More than two seasons had passed before a few fathers and husbands either heard the whispers or wondered why a skinny, uneducated boy with such a scarcity of skills should be so much in demand throughout the town. Thus threatened, the confident lad decided he had accomplished all he could there and set off for new opportunities. Thus he came to Lancashire.

When he arrived in the coastal county, now a man of eighteen, he decided it would be prudent to establish friendships with men before he began his conquest of the village ladies. He reasoned that the local tavern would be the right spot to engage with peers. A single inquiry was sufficient to lead him there. From the outside, it was nondescript, a simple structure of stone and wood with a few windows through which little more than the glow of oil lamps was visible.

No heads turned upon his entry, chiefly because a disturbance was in progress within. Two men had squared off against one, and while Matty was unaware of the three men's identities or the nature of their disagreement, he instinctively sympathized with the lone combatant. For now, however, he stood still and stared along with the tavern's other patrons.

No blows had yet been struck; rather, the three men were shouting at each other, although their crouched postures suggested wild animals preparing to attack. As he listened, Matty picked up clues as to the offense that caused this row.

"I tell you, it was not my doing," said the lone man, clearly the one in the more defensive position. "Who am I, that Lord Barnard would heed my advice?"

"Then what explains his sudden change of heart?" challenged the taller of the two aggressors. "Two years in succession Lord Barnard hired Phillip and me to be his guides, and paid us handsomely. We've prepared already for the next hunt. Now, the day before we are to leave, we are told he has hired you in our stead. Tell us why, Quentin Wainwright, or your blood will mark the place that you stand!"

The lone combatant, a rugged, fine-looking young man whom Matty now knew was named Quentin, had apparently had enough of the accusations and decided he had little to lose by going on the offensive.

"Hear this, you ignorant swine," spoke Quentin. "A blind man can see that I am a superior shot than your brother. In fact, a blind man *is* a better shot than the two of you sops combined. Lord Barnard knows it, and now so does everyone present. Come at me if you dare, but know that I've a fist for each of you."

And the two offended men did just that. Phillip came in first and was easily brought down by Quentin with a swift blow to the chin. The other, more talkative one had a slight advantage in that he could attack while Quentin's momentum was still directed at his brother. And indeed he landed a punch to the side of Quentin's head. The force threw Quentin off balance but he was able to right himself and come back at the taller man. The two grappled and wrestled, each seeking an advantage of space and position so that a forceful blow could be struck.

Meanwhile, Phillip began to sit up. Rubbing his chin and seeing his brother in close combat with Quentin, he clambered to his feet. Matty saw him reach into his coat and withdraw a pistol. At that moment, Quentin created enough separation that he was able to deliver two punches in rapid succession to the nose and cheek of Phillip's brother. The taller man reeled and struck his head against the edge of the bar, knocking him unconscious. Blood immediately began to flow from his nostrils and forehead as he collapsed to the floor.

With that, Phillip raised his armed hand and took aim at Quentin. Instinctively, Matty reached for a bottle from the table he stood adjacent to, and hurled it at Phillip, standing no more than two body lengths away. Matty's aim was true and the whiskey-filled weapon hit the back of Phillip's head with a sickening thud. The would-be assassin fell forward, his firearm dropping and hitting the floor just ahead of him. Quentin rushed over and grabbed the pistol, tucked it within the belt of his trousers, and then dragged the two men out of the tavern and onto the street.

By now, all heads had turned in Matty's direction. And if the response was not quite what David received upon slaying the Philistine with his rock and kerchief, he was made to feel welcome. The gentleman whose bottle Matty had thrown ordered a replacement and offered Matty the first shot from it. A few introductions were made, although some viewed him suspiciously – not without reason, of course; after all, his first public act in the town was one of violence. This was not the impression Matty had hoped to make in his new dwelling-place.

Some minutes had passed before Quentin returned. Having taken the brothers outside, he called then for a constable. When one arrived and took the luckless pair away, Quentin went directly to wash up and compose himself. Upon his return, he ordered two drinks from Richardson and walked towards Matty, a dram of whisky in each hand.

"Sir, I am in your debt," said Quentin, offering one of the glasses to his unknown ally. "My name is Quentin Wainwright and I would be honored if you would accept this drink, a momentary refreshment, along with my unending friendship and loyalty."

"Matthew Musgrave," said he, accepting the gift. "I am called Matty by my friends and Little Musgrave by my lovers. My enemies have called me many other names."

Quentin smiled. "In that case, *Matty*, your enemies are my enemies, as you have already taken my enemies as yours. Come, let us sit and drink and get to know each other."

The handsome pair sat down and talked for many hours, until they had outlasted all the other company and the proprietor forced them to leave. On the way out, Quentin asked Matty where he lived. Matty explained that he had only arrived in town that day and had yet to secure lodging for himself. Quentin insisted then that Matty come share his home. Matty accepted and stayed for several weeks until Quentin introduced him to Erickson the printer. In that time, the two men became fast friends. In Quentin, Matty finally felt he had the brother he had lost; moreover, he had actually been able to save this brother's life. In

Matty, Quentin found a spirit that was as contagious as it was unquenchable.

It should, then, have been a pleasant sight for Matty when, emerging from the house after his meeting with Lord Barnard, he spied Quentin and Alexandra speaking with each other. In truth, however, Matty's mind still reeled with the information Lord Barnard had given him. He wished to be alone with his confused thoughts, to wrestle with the prospect of a prestigious new future, of a station above and beyond that of his family, his friends, and his lovers.

Instead, he would have to engage in conversation, though it was with two people he cared for very deeply. Knowing he could not say anything about Lord Barnard's offer, at least not until he had digested it in his mind and settled on a response or resolution, he forced himself to adopt the carefree tenor and attitude that people expected of him and for which they loved him.

"Ah, Matty," called Quentin, "just the fellow I seek. I have a favor to ask of you."

"I granted you a favor the day I met you," Matty replied. "Has that not proven sufficient?"

"I believe it is time to come clean on that score," said Quentin. "The fact is that even at point blank range,

Phillip could never have hit me. Therefore, you didn't really save my life at all."

"Perhaps not," countered Matty, "but certainly I have improved it."

Alexandra laughed while Quentin smiled and nodded, and then he continued. "Quite so, Little Musgrave, quite so. But in all earnestness, I must ask you: would you be willing to take my place among the pace-eggers on Easter Sunday?"

"Pace-eggers? Bah, they're but beggars."

"And are you now a nobleman, Matty Musgrove?" asked Alexandra. The question caused Matty to flinch, but he righted himself quickly.

"A beggar begs for what he cannot get for himself," explained Matty. "All I need I can acquire through my own means."

"Aye," said Alexandra, with a knowing nod, "and you are a persuasive one, indeed."

"Why are you not engaging in the festivities this year?" Matty asked Quentin.

"Your master has scheduled a hunting trip over the holiday and, once again, he wants my eyes and my guns."

"I would like to help you, you know I would. But I must refuse. This holiday I feel the need to stay free of obligations. Please understand."

"I do, my friend," said Quentin. "I, too, wish I could be a passive spectator. But Lord Barnard is also a persuasive one. I must find someone to take my place. I was to portray the Old Tosspot this year. Therefore, I must bid you farewell for now. Miss Alexandra. Matty." Bowing to each in turn, Quentin adjusted his coat and walked away.

"What troubles you, Matty?" inquired Alexandra once Quentin was well beyond earshot.

"Why do you think I am troubled?" replied Matty.

"Because I know you well, far better than you know yourself."

This may well have been true. Shortly after Matty began working for Erickson, he made Alexandra's acquaintance. She was in town purchasing soap for the Barnards' washing. Matty was instantly smitten. A lovely face, to be sure, yet in her posture and gait she clearly also was confident and strong. The sinuous curls of her hair, her large round eyes, held him transfixed. And even through layers of inconvenient garments, he could tell she had the figure of Venus.

Alexandra noticed him as well. In fact, she had heard of him already. A friend of hers had enjoyed a tryst with him once in Erickson's stable. Yet she allowed Matty to introduce himself to her. She betrayed no knowledge of him and gave off an impression of polite indifference. This merely served as bellows to the flame that began to consume his insides. He asked if he might take her on a walk sometime. She replied that she was busy but that he was invited to run errands for her if he cared to be a gentleman.

And so, for about three weeks, Alexandra fetched no water, bought no soap, and carried no baskets of clean laundry up the steps to the Barnards' porch. Matty came by every day to see what she needed. And he did so willingly, for no woman had ever cast such a spell over him without first having shared her treasures. Finally, she agreed to go on the walk with Matty and, as she expected, little actual walking was ultimately achieved. Yet a bond was indeed forged between the two.

For Matty, Alexandra was a lover to be respected. Knowledgeable and responsive, she distinguished between desire and need, could not be forced into anything, and did nothing out of obligation. Her father, a fisherman, had once arranged a marriage for her; the prospective groom's father, however, had tried to get to know his future daughter-in-law a little too intimately before the ceremony. She resisted with fingers to his eyes and a knee to his genitals. He then called off the wedding and from that time forward Alexandra decided that she would control her own body and destiny.

So Matty and Alexandra became lovers, yet, to their mutual pleasure, both rejected the shackles of exclusivity. Freedom was the watchword of their faith, and the virtue they most valued. So it was that the topic of freedom surfaced in their present conversation.

"So tell me what is occupying your mind so," said Alexandra. "I can tell something is the matter, because your dour demeanor is in stark contrast with your usual vivaciousness," she continued with a smile.

"You do know me well, Alexandra," said Matty. "And I know you. Neither of us was bred for a life of comfort or order, were we? We seek what we desire and ignore the rest, do we not? Our lives are about courage, not consequences."

"I'll not argue your words, Matty," she said, "not yet. But I do not understand your point."

Matty paused, his lips pressed tightly together. He looked down, inhaled deeply and exhaled slowly. Then he looked back at her. "Alexandra, I cannot help being who I am. And I like being who I am. I am responsible only to myself and to my employer. And that's the beautiful thing about you and me. We are free beings, and we shouldn't allow anyone to change us, either for good or ill. Don't you agree?"

"Well, Matty, I still don't know from whence comes this curious questioning. But you are wrong. You aren't free, and though you act irresponsibly sometimes you do have responsibilities and you perform them admirably. We both rely on others for shelter and a wage.

"Furthermore," she continued, "you and I are different. As a woman, there are consequences to my behavior. My body changes from moon to moon. And I cannot go and chase my fancy whenever I please. They talk about you, Matty Musgrave, and your reputation grows. It is that of a rake, a rogue, a rascal. But any word about me and mine is one of shame and disparagement."

Matty stared at his feet, uncomfortable at Alexandra's frank testimony, yet unable to dispute it.

"Neither of us are free," she went on, "but you are more free than I. And besides, I don't think you are capable of changing or being changed. I say that with affection, of course. So whatever is troubling you, I beg you to dismiss it. There is no one quite like you, Matty, so I pity the person who would try to make you into something else."

"Something you have never tried to do, my dear sweet Alexandra," said Matty earnestly and with gratitude. "You truly are a blessing to me. I should like to kiss you here, in the open, where all could see. But my horses beckon and Darnell is somewhere about, so I must leave you now. I thank you for your concern. Until we meet again."

And with that, he turned towards the stable. Alexandra, watching him go, felt she had said too much, yet there still was much she needed to say but couldn't. It was hard to love Matty, and harder still sometimes to have his love. Furthermore, this talk of changing and freedom upset her. Though not for his sake, but for her own.

Chapter 5

Matty's face was handsome, all knew it was true. Most, upon first seeing it, thought it the face of Adonis himself. When Lord Barnard first gazed upon it, though, he was struck not simply by its beauty but by its resemblance to a boy he knew in school.

Lord Barnard had three older sisters, and they and their mother delighted in finally having a baby boy to play with. His father, whose own father before him had been one of the founders of the village and was appointed to serve as its first governor, was a strong yet gentle and capable man who would have been as happy to work as a simple carpenter as to ascend to nobility. As the elder Barnard's responsibilities took him away from home for extended periods, Lord Barnard grew close to his mother, a kind yet illiterate woman whose breads and cakes were known to people a day's ride from the village. Within the village proper, she was also well-regarded as a compassionate and capable midwife.

Though his father was well known and his family well to do, the adolescent Barnard had few friends. He was not overtly ostracized by his school peers, but the other boys did whisper about him. Some thought him strange, perhaps a tad fey. He didn't go in for rough and tumble play, fretted about getting his clothing soiled, was quiet and enjoyed spending time alone to read and to contemplate. He was, quite simply, different.

Just as the other boys wondered about him, he also wondered about them.

Why must they be so boisterous all the time, he ruminated. *Have they no self-control? Is this how commoners raise their offspring? They are like chickens trying to elude the slaughterer. Even if they were to have me as their friend, I should not know how nor wish to engage in their frivolities.*

Mutual distaste eventually evolved into mutual dislike. Except for one lad, Peter Williams, who arrived when the boys were twelve years old.

Peter was handsome like Matty, with thick dark hair and exotic features. Born of an English father and a West Indian mother, he was darker than their peers and also the target of their teasing. Lord Barnard and Peter took comfort in each other, shared their dreams and fears, and swore love and loyalty to each other. But just a little over a year after he'd arrived in the village, Peter contracted a virus. He had a high fever for more than a week, could hold down neither food nor water, and died.

Lord Barnard was inconsolable, so much so that the other boys actually began to show some compassion for him, inviting him to join their activities. But he couldn't bear to forgive his tormentors. Through grade school and even while at University, he had no true friend who could compare with Peter, either in looks or fealty. By the time he reached adulthood, Lord Barnard's social circle, such as it was, comprised business associates exclusively: serious men who valued wisdom and success.

If he was aloof around boys growing up, he was terribly shy around girls and had never so much as held one's hand until he took his bride's during their wedding ceremony. With Lord Barnard nearing the age of thirty, and no prospects in sight, his father arranged the marriage – "You are too old to remain single," the elder Barnard told his reluctant son – and the day of the nuptials marked only the third time he had met her.

Lady Barnard was from northwest Sheffield, and she came with a modest dowry: five sacks of freshly milled grain, seven pewter goblets, a dozen chickens, and two goats. Fair and intelligent, her fitness to be a wife and mother were assumed, yet she always had her doubts. She had willingly served her father, but her new husband was more serious, less handsome, and certainly less familiar to her. However, she was raised to obey and she was prepared to uphold those expectations dutifully.

On their wedding night, the bed they shared for the first time shook, though more from their collective unease than from gymnastic exertions of passion. Neither had experience in this sort of thing, and it went badly. No words were spoken between them that night (there was nothing he *could* say, and nothing she *should* say). The next night they tried again and managed to couple, though only for a few minutes before it had reached its conclusion. A third time took place two nights later, and for the first time Lady Barnard had a glimmer that the act needn't be merely functional – yet for Lord Barnard, it was unwelcome duty.

He had sensed for some time that he was not like the other men he knew who yearned for a woman's flesh and spoke of their desire and their exploits, and often with braggart tones. He did not understand its appeal; the whole thing seemed messy, intimidating, and distasteful. He found greater satisfaction engaging in work and study, two areas where he generally did not come into contact with the other gender.

Lord Barnard had been quite comfortable in his virginity – not proud, necessarily, but also not eager to explore the alternative. When he married Lady Barnard, however, suddenly there were expectations, both between the married couple and among their respective families. He was expected to sire children, heirs to the family name and estate. After the first few weeks of their marriage, however, Lord Barnard realized he couldn't fulfill the duty of a husband with any degree of frequency or skill. He hoped each time for a successful issue that would lead to a pregnancy.

One child, he said to himself, *and I'll no longer have to play this charade.*

But no child came. To be fair, few were the attempts to conceive, and after a while each attempt had to be preceded by a few shots of whisky. This did not increase the rate of success, but it made Lord Barnard more relaxed and less put off by the chore. Lady Barnard shared the desire for a child yet also had managed to experience some degree of pleasure from the act – by sheer dint of pressure and friction she was brought near some invisible plateau she yearned to leap onto, but sadly the experience was never sustained sufficiently for her to reach that elusive point. Thus, she was increasingly distressed by her husband's lack of interest.

It is not surprising, then, that she came to view herself as unattractive, or as lacking the skill, sensuality, or seductive powers that women with faithful, fruitful husbands must possess.

Soon Lord Barnard took up hunting as an excuse to spend time away from home. He organized parties of friends and business acquaintances, and hired guides to lead him and his party to distant grounds rich with wild game. In warmer months, the men would bathe together in a lake, both upon rising and after the day's hunt. There was mischief as always happens when boys and men are together, but gradually Lord Barnard began having feelings he could not define. He had no example to allow him to say, *This that I know exists, is true as well with me*. These feelings troubled him, and he was mortified that his body could betray his feelings when he watched the other men swim and romp.

One day when Darnell was ill and confined to his quarters, Lord Barnard went himself to the village general store to purchase gunpowder. There, he met the young clerk, Quentin Wainwright. Quentin talked of his skill and experience hunting in the farthest reaches of the county. Lord Barnard listened intently yet could not look the man in the eye. Instead, he focused on Quentin's mouth, which seemed ever to be shaped into a smile, and the lips, the way they formed vowels and consonants, became moist with spittle, and rested with the upper jutting ever so slightly forward of the lower.

Lord Barnard had hired two brothers as guides already, but with fumbling language he offered Quentin an amount equal to the total of what the two brothers were due to receive if the clerk would agree to serve as his guide on a trip leaving the very next day. The money was too attractive to refuse, and his employer granted him the time away from the store purely because it was Lord Barnard who had conveyed the offer.

Though Lord Barnard hired Quentin time and again, their only physical contact was a handshake and maybe a platonic embrace following a particularly exciting or challenging kill. Lord Barnard even took to rising early so that he could bathe alone while the others were asleep. He was content to view beauty rather than partake of it, like an art lover who wields not a brush himself.

In spite of his friendship with Quentin, Lord Barnard never made Matty's acquaintance until that day at Erickson's auction. While Quentin was a very fine-looking man, Matty was truly a sight to behold. It was not just his face that put certain people into a spell, but his voice, his hair, his build, his personality. People were drawn to him the way flowers reach for the sun's life-enabling rays.

Certainly, few women could resist his allure; some men felt the same.

In the first year of Matty's employment, Lord Barnard had become all but smitten with him. He would look out of his window daily to watch him work in the stable and cross the yard on the way to town. Still, Lord Barnard did not view Matty as a potential lover, but rather as the son he had yearned for, the son who not only would be his heir and companion – and thus would always be near to him – but who in so being would also remove the constant pressure on Lord Barnard to have a child and thus continue having sexual relations with his wife.

None of this Lady Barnard suspected. To her, his inability to become aroused was simply part of a larger pattern of being distant and unpleasant. When they first were wed, she was expected to serve. As his wealth and position improved, and servants were hired, she no longer had a role. And without a role – be it homemaker, mother, or temptress – she was losing any sense of her own identity and worth. Wine dulled the sadness associated with this loss, but did nothing to restore what was slipping steadily away from her.

And so, as Lord Barnard entered her room and sent Darnell out, Lady Barnard, still embracing the notion that the house servant finds her attractive, steeled herself for she knew this small, fragile bubble of good feeling would soon be pricked.

Facing his wife, Lord Barnard remained silent for several moments after Darnell left the room. He waited, in fact, until the servant left the house. When he heard the door downstairs close, Lord Barnard turned to look out the window, the same one through which Lady Barnard had earlier gazed. Satisfied that Darnell was beyond hearing range, he swung around to engage Lady Barnard. But she was not looking in his direction. She, too, had turned away and was facing her bed on the opposite wall.

Thus it was for this married couple, for little had they shared at all these ten years. Days could pass and the only time they would interact would be at breakfast and supper. Of course, Lord Barnard had business and other interests that took him away to various locales, some requiring a journey of a fortnight or more. Yet whether he was far away or in the next room, Lady Barnard was more often than not sure to be alone, an unbound hostage inside an inhospitable house.

"I'll not having you commingling with the villagers," he would say when she expressed a desire to go into town. "You are far too fair. You would come down with the ague before nightfall." Many such excuses were tendered, yet in reality Lord Barnard was concerned about what she might reveal to others about their lives, most specifically about him. And so came this morning's rant.

"I am leaving on a hunting trip this Thursday," Lord Barnard said, "and will be gone four days."

"I know," Lady Barnard replied. "You've told me."

"You will have to miss Easter services this year," he continued, "but I will ask Reverend Collins if he might drop by and offer you the Sacrament here."

"I have no intention of missing Easter services. Mr. McDougall is making a bonnet for me."

"That is of no matter," he said, his voice a little louder, a little higher pitched. "I am leaving and you are staying, and that is all."

"Why must you leave before Easter and why stay past it? You are my husband. You belong by my side. We should be going to church together."

"You belong where I say you will belong," Lord Barnard shouted. "When I want you beside me, you shall be by my side. When I want you away, you shall be away. And when I want you to stay at home, you shall stay at home." (These last five words were rendered staccato.)

Lord Barnard began to march swiftly out the door, then stopped and looked back at his now-weeping wife. "I will not have you cavorting about the town, gossiping like a mad crone," he yelled still louder. "Only when I desire your conversation will you speak. And when I do not, you will be silent. And in all cases, you will be here in this house, and not among the coarse commoners in the village. That is my last word on the subject!"

Then Lord Barnard walked out and slammed the door closed. Lady Barnard sat upon her bed, her head in her hands, her tears wetting her wrists. As sad as she was, she was assured now of one thing: it was not her fault.

Chapter 6

It was two days prior to Easter and the town was astir with excitement and activity. At church, the Reverend Sanford Collins was reviewing his sermon notes. Not yet thirty years old, he wore tightly cropped whiskers on his chin, keeping the space between his lips and nose hairless.

As a youth, against the advice of his parents and the village physician, he had embraced his younger brother, then near-mad with a raging fever. Unexpectedly, the boy's fever broke that night and the superstitious villagers were convinced that Almighty God had worked through young Sanford's hands directly. Thus, the precocious lad, a believer in any case, was coaxed into serving as the area's spiritual leader, though he had no pastoral training and never had undertaken Bible study of any depth.

His theme, predictably, would be rebirth and resurrection. He would focus this year on the idea that when we are reborn, blissful in Eternal Afterlife, there are things that we will lose.

In becoming perfected, he'd written, *we will become less than we are currently, not more. Just as Jesus lost his physical form and returned incorporeal, all those who are saved have taken from them any number of things –*

negative traits, sinful impulses, bad habits, unholy urges –
that had weighed down their mortal lives on earth.

The young cleric's key point, then, was that people should let go of those things now – things such as lust, possessions, hatred, and greed – that eventually will be taken from them anyway.

Do not desire things that degrade human personality, he had written, *such as flesh and power. Live more simply and spiritually. Then when your time is due, your transformation will be that much more swift and sure.*

In the field adjacent to the church, Mr. McDougall was selecting the flowers he would cut for Lady Barnard's Easter bonnet. In addition to the peonies and paperwhites, the bonnet would be adorned with a lace trim that his wife was making by hand. The Lady's bonnet was the one commission he anticipated most each year. She came out in public so rarely that to be seen in a creation of his would surely keep the women of the town clamoring for his flowers and crafts until the first frost settled on the ground.

Meanwhile, Quentin had succeeded in finding someone to replace him among the pace-eggers, and the troupe were attending to their costumes, practicing their songs and lines, and planning their route. From a room in the back of the tavern where they had been gathering the last several nights, passers-by on the street could hear the absurd verses sung in rowdy fashion, starting always with the first:

> *Here's one, two, three jolly lads all in one mind*
> *We have come a pace-egging and we hope you'll*
> *prove kind*
> *We hope you'll prove kind with your eggs and*
> *strong beer*
> *For we'll come no more nigh you until the next*
> *year.*

As for himself, Quentin was checking surveys of the surrounding areas and stocking up on gunpowder for the next day's departure. Lord Barnard had told him that he didn't wish to go far, and that he should make sure that Darnell knew the precise location of their camp.

Unbeknownst to Quentin, Lord Barnard was planning to enforce his order to his wife that she not attend church on Easter Sunday. He would ask Darnell, as yet also unaware of the plan, to find and inform him if his wife left the house that day. Of course, Lord Barnard was unaware that Darnell had already accepted his wife's invitation to serve as her escort to church.

For his part, Matty had spent the morning with the horses, preparing them for the hunting trip. Freshly cleaned and polished were the saddles, bits, and bridles. He had bathed and brushed the animals, and filled sacks with oats. When the sun had reached its highest point in the sky and the warmth had filled the stable, Matty emerged to obtain a drink of water for himself. He walked over to the well near the center of the property and began to work the pump. He had perspired heavily in the stable, and his shirt clung to his shoulders and back, constricting his movements. He stopped and removed his shirt, then went back to the pump, more eager than ever to draw a ladle of earth-cooled water.

It was at this moment that Lady Barnard drew closer again to her window. This time, her gaze caught Matty's form squarely. She gasped audibly, half in surprise at seeing a seminude man in the yard, and half in admiration for the sheer aesthetic quality of the specimen he was. She didn't recognize his face – a face such as his she would not have forgotten had she seen it before.

Though Matty had worked and lived on her property for more than a year, Lady Barnard's ignorance of him should not be a complete surprise. She despised the smell of horses, feared them since seeing her youngest sister, then ten, thrown from one, breaking her arm. As such, Lady Barnard never spent time around the stable (in this, she and Darnell were alike, though Darnell's dislike of Matty also contributed to his avoidance of that structure).

Being confined to the house – she tended to further restrict herself to her room – Lady Barnard looked out on the yard often, though not so much to observe or notice people; rather, she typically focused on the expanse of the property and the woods and ocean beyond, or of the horizon itself, the boundless vistas she envied simply because they could not be contained. They reminded her of the places she had read of in books and dreamed of visiting in real life, a life that for all her wealth and station never had materialized.

Yet here was cause for shortening and sharpening her focus. She continued to watch Matty as he drew water and drank it, then drew more to splash on his face and dump on his head. Streams of water slid down his face and provided a cool caress to his muscular, hairless chest and stomach. Though he was heated by his exertion, and the day was at its warmest, it still was early spring and not summer; it was not, therefore, a hot day. And this was why the cold water on his bare torso brought a chill to Matty, causing his flesh to rise in countless tiny protuberances. This, too, was noticed and admired by Lady Barnard, aided with a spyglass she previously had used only to see stars more clearly.

Matty was unaware he was being watched; or else, he was so accustomed to being noticed that he didn't check to see whose eyes may be on him. Quenched and cooled, he replaced his shirt and ran his fingers through his dripping hair, pushing the strands behind his ears and away from his face. This last look afforded to the Lady triggered a sensation within her that she had not experienced before without first having been touched intimately. Aware as she was that there might be more to lovemaking than she had yet to experience first-hand, Lady Barnard sensed now that this man – dirty, no doubt malodorous, at the very least from a lowly station – might hold the key to her physical fulfillment and happiness.

This thought so held her imagination that she turned away from the window and stared at her wall, a silent witness that could only assent to her apparent resolve to know this man. To do so would require two things to happen. First, Lord Barnard must leave. Then, she must do likewise. It was always daring to disobey her husband; now, she felt there were greater consequences in continuing to dismiss her own needs and desires.

No longer looking out the window, Lady Barnard did not see Matty walk away from the well and leave the property. His destination was Quentin's home, to bid him good luck and farewell before his hunting trip with Lord Barnard. The walk was not long, though it was pleasant for a man popular as he. As he passed, women turned their heads. Men he had regaled at the tavern called out to him. He had been much more successful integrating himself into the community here in Lancashire than he had been before in other places. Though just as active, he had learned to be more discreet. He valued his friendships with men and endeavored to maintain them, even those with whose wives he had lain.

Upon arriving at Quentin's, Matty saw his good friend sitting beneath the shade of a willow tree. He was polishing a brass horn, such as the type used by soldiers and hunters to sound the call to arms when chasing their respective prey.

"Ho there," said Matty.

"Welcome, my friend," said Quentin, waving Matty over to join him on the ground. "May I offer you some shade from the midday sun?"

"Exactly what I was craving," Matty replied. He sat down next to Quentin. "That's a fine horn."

"A gift from your master it is," said Quentin, offering it to Matty for his inspection. "I'm planning on bringing it with me tomorrow. So what brings you here?"

"I wanted to wish you well on your journey," said Matty, as he handled the horn and thought of the gifts he had also received from his employer, "and to say I shall miss you over the holiday."

"And I you, Matty," Quentin responded. "I would rather join you in hunting fair ladies in their finest dress after church than in bagging foxes and pheasants with Barnard and his cronies."

"Never to worry, Quentin, for I shall be sure to capture and feast upon such a grand trophy that she would have satisfied the both of us."

"I'm sure you shall, Matty, but it is not your manner to leave behind any morsels for less-skillful hunters," Quentin said with a laugh.

"Then I shall think of you when I take my spoils," said Matty. "Tell me, who is in Lord Barnard's party?"

"Aside from he and I, there is a chap by the name of Finster, I believe. Barnard said he was his solicitor. He is also taking Dennis Upham the tailor and his banker friend Thomas something. That is all, a small party for the first trip of the year."

At the word "solicitor" Matty stopped listening. *So, it is to be set legal this very trip*, he thought to himself. *Away from me, giving me no chance to refuse.*

"Has Lord Barnard said anything about why he invited his solicitor?" asked Matty.

"Not to me. Why?"

"Nothing really," replied Matty.

"Are you all right?" asked Quentin. "You've suddenly turned white as lamb's fleece."

"No, yes, I'm fine, I was just curious is all."

"Well, your master, he's a strange one. I don't bother asking him anything about what he does and why he does it."

"Strange?" Matty asked. "How so?"

"Well, I don't know exactly. It's just that…well, he…he's rather standoff-ish, you know?"

"No, actually. I find him rather brusque myself, though he shows me much kindness. How exactly do you mean?"

"I can't find the words," Quentin replied, "but he tends to sort of…stare at people. Me, sometimes. You, of course, I've noticed that, everyone has. But other fellows as well. Sure, he engages in conversation, he takes part in the hunt. But he never relaxes. That's what it is. He's very intense, doesn't joke, laugh, smoke, anything. Just stands apart and stares a lot of the time. Makes me rather uncomfortable."

"Why do you think he does it?" asked Matty.

"Well, I don't know. I don't know what he means by it. What is he like at his home? Does he just stare at his wife?"

"Perhaps. Alexandra thinks they don't do much together, personal-like," said Matty.

"You should ask your friend Darnell there. I'm sure he knows what's what."

"Oh yes, my 'friend' Darnell, we're close as cousins we are," laughed Matty. "He says as little as possible to me, addresses me only when he has to."

"Well, get him drunk and see if that brings his speech out," said Quentin. "I wouldn't mind knowing what goes on in there. And what doesn't."

Matty rose to his feet and handed Quentin back his gift. "My advice to you," he said, "is to put it out of your mind and rest well tonight. For I expect you to slay something particularly large and nasty on your trip, and I will look forward to hearing you tell of your kill. Godspeed, good friend." With that, Matty and Quentin embraced and went back to minding their respective tasks.

Returning to the Barnard estate, Matty mulled over Quentin's suggestion. While he was half-joshing, it was a sound idea. Matty needed to know some things about their lives if he was going to become a part of it. And if the testimony was decidedly unfavorable, then Matty would have to do something to ensure that this adoption of sorts would not play out. He could run away, but there was always the risk of recapture. As well, even if successful he likely would lose not only his livelihood but also his friends, Quentin and dear Alexandra.

Of course, he had no fear of starting over again in a new county, he'd done it before, but he had a feeling of belonging here that was not true of his previous surroundings.

Considering two poles of possibilities, one benign and the other outrageous, talking Lord Barnard out of the arrangement was unlikely to be successful while murdering him would not render Matty free. His only reasonable alternative was to make himself appear unworthy to be a nobleman's heir. How to accomplish this was a challenge, since he didn't consider himself worthy already.

What should I do? he thought. *Curse and be drunk all the day? Do some petty theft? Take something of value to him?*

No, he reasoned, *I must not let my mind race ahead of me. First, I must find a way to encourage Darnell to accompany me to the tavern one night. Then I can ply him with several pints and let the gossip pour out like draught ale from a keg. I shall attend to this tonight, after supper.*

And yet the very thought of the detestable page brought forth the outrageous realization that since Matty would become the *de facto* son of Lord Barnard, Darnell would be obligated to serve the former stable hand as well! Darnell taking orders from Matty – surely neither man would abide by such a thing for long.

Arriving on the grounds of the Barnard residence, Matty was so consumed by his thoughts and plans that he didn't notice Alexandra wave to him. She saw him preoccupied and worried for him. All men are entitled to their moods, but Matty – in so many ways – was not just another man. She had long expected that his boundless enthusiasm for a life that held little future promise (he was limited in trade skills, after all, and his looks wouldn't last him another ten years) was a masquerade. A magnificent one to be sure, yet no disguise, no matter how pleasing, could do aught but suffocate its wearer in time.

Many were the moments that Alexandra sought to peel back his mask and gaze upon his true visage. Yet she knew that would violate the understanding the two had with each other. Each was entitled to privacy, freedom, space. Alexandra respected and abided by this unspoken agreement chiefly because she craved it for herself; yet to what useful end it served was a question more troubling to her when it concerned Matty's inherent mysteries.

She remembered his arrival in town well. Never had a sober man been so forward with her. She'd have thought him rude but for his large, kind eyes that focused so intently on hers, and the genuine pleasantness with which he made his introduction. Her feet were not so easily swept off the ground, however, and she saw that she could use his keen interest in her to her advantage. She made him her servant in essence, thinking that no man so intent on establishing relations with a woman would bear to wait and wade through countless tasks simply to prove his worth.

In fact, few men would, and while Matty could have been one of them, he was not suffering cold nights alone while he waited for Alexandra to accept his entreaties. Alexandra found this out, though not until after they had first consummated their mutual desire for each other. Rather than feeling hurt or betrayed, it attracted him to her all the more. Not because she favored rogues as a rule, but because he was so certain of what he wanted and knew how to get it. And the more he got, the more he seemed to want, yet without the desperation and overt deception that the insatiably needy typically demonstrate. His very confidence and independence was attractive to her, though in weaker moments she allowed herself to consider a life they could lead together.

The sun now was setting and thick ashen clouds confederated in the sky. With the wind rising and the darkness thus accelerated, it was clear that the night would be filled with the sound and scent of rainfall. As Alexandra looked to the rugs and linens on the clothesline, clean and dry but threatened by the advancing weather, Darnell emerged from the house.

"May I help you bring in the wash?" he asked, seeing both the foreboding sky and the vulnerable work of Alexandra's hands.

"Yes, thank you," she replied.

"Lord Barnard will leave tomorrow for his hunting trip," said Darnell as he pulled down an ivory-hued oval rug.

"That is what I hear," said Alexandra. "The poor Lady will be left alone on Easter."

"Without her husband, yes, but not alone," Darnell replied in hushed tones. "She has asked me to escort her to church services on Sunday morning."

"Well, well, Darnell. Your station is rising. And her husband approved of this arrangement?"

"I believe he is unaware," replied Darnell, "and that is how it should remain."

Alexandra smiled coyly as she bent down to lift her wash basket. As she rose and straightened her back, she got suddenly dizzy, dropping the basket and nearly collapsing rearwards. Darnell dropped the rug he was holding, making it dirtier in seconds than it had been before Alexandra expended so much energy beating and washing it. He lunged to catch her as she reeled, and he held her in his protective embrace, his pulse racing both from the unexpected crisis and the fact that he finally had Alexandra in his arms.

"Alexandra, what is the matter? Are you ill?" he managed to speak through his gasping throat.

Tired, weakened, slightly nauseous, yet otherwise feeling normal after a long day of work, Alexandra was more embarrassed than alarmed. She accepted his arms around her for a moment, then patted his shoulder and gently pushed against it, signaling that she was ready and wanting to stand independently.

"Yes," she said with a slight wooziness to her voice. "I mean, no, I'm fine. I'm so sorry, Darnell. Thank you for catching me. I just had a dizzy spell."

"Are you sure you're well?"

"Yes, I'm fine, it's just…." She paused; seeing the rug on the ground, she exploited the chance to change the subject. "I see my laundry is not finished after all."

"I'm sorry I dropped the rug, Alexandra. I was just so startled when I saw you faint." He guided her to the steps of the house. "Come sit here. You must rest. Shall I send for the doctor?"

"No, Darnell. Really I'm fine. It's just dizziness. We must get the rest of the washing into the house. I thought I felt a drop."

"You stay here. I'll bring in the laundry."

"That's very kind of you, Darnell," said Alexandra, grateful for the momentary rest. "I'm sorry to burden you."

Darnell sat down next to her. Emboldened by their accidental embrace, he took her hands in his and looked into her eyes. "Alexandra, it is no burden to want to take care of you. And if it is, then I shall gladly bear it for a lifetime. You are a strong woman, but I can be strong for you as well. If only you will allow me."

Alexandra looked down at his hands grasping hers. His hands, his man's hands, were softer and cleaner than her own.

He doesn't work with his hands, she thought. *He works with his nodding head and with his scurrying feet, attending to the whims and wishes of the Barnards. It is not manual labor…but it is not easy work, either*, she acknowledged.

There were advantages to being a house servant, of course, but the job required a great deal of skill, tact, and resourcefulness. She knew she would not unhesitatingly trade places with him, nor could she think of others in the Barnards' employ who would want to hear what he hears, know what he knows, and be as trusting and discreet as his position requires.

Trusting. Discreet. Yes, Darnell was these, and these she felt she would need at this time. She looked up at him and as rain began to fall intermittently, she began slowly to speak.

"Darnell. I know what you say is true, and I do appreciate it. You have a good heart and you are a good friend. I have burdened you with duty and now I would like to burden you with knowledge."

"I don't understand," said Darnell.

Alexandra paused, then spoke softly.

"Darnell, I have a secret and it's a shameful one. No, that's not quite true. Yet it…. What I mean is, I don't feel ashamed but others would think it a scandal and would judge me so. I haven't wanted to tell anyone, and of course I'm not sure it is a fact, but if what I feel to be true is true, then my condition will become obvious before long and I will need more help."

Darnell remained quiet. Their eyes remained locked. His hands tightened their grip on hers, prodding her to continue.

"I think I am with child, Darnell."

"Is Matty the father?" asked Darnell.

"It is likely," she replied.

"Does he know?" he asked.

"No," said Alexandra. "And as you said before, that is how it should remain. At least until I know for sure that I am pregnant."

"Do you believe he does not want the child?" asked Darnell.

"I don't know," she said. "I don't know how or whether to broach the subject with him. He is a free spirit, as you know, and though he may love me and may even love the child, I don't think that husband and father are roles he is eager to play."

"Then let me play them, Alexandra," said Darnell. "All that I have pledged you before I pledge again, plus this: I will have your child as my own. I will love and raise and teach that child, and that child will know me as its father, and you as its beloved mother, and we all shall be one family.

"You have denied me repeatedly, Alexandra," he continued. "And never have I lost my desire for you. No one need know that you are unmarried and with child. We can marry soon and preserve your honor. Your child need not be a bastard. You must consent to be my wife."

"Darnell," said Alexandra, "I don't want to marry out of necessity, if I even ever want to marry at all. At present, I am weak and tired, and you are kind and honest. It would be too easy to accept your offer right now. Please give me some more time."

Darnell released her hands and nodded silently. She grabbed his hands back, then kissed him on the cheek.

"Please know that I am grateful for your affection," she said. "And please know my affection for you increases."

Darnell blushed and smiled. He felt he finally had broken through. Certainly there was added urgency because of her condition. Yet she had admitted her affection for him. With Lady Barnard on his arm on Sunday, and the prospect of Alexandra as his wife, his spirits were high and his confidence strong. He felt like…well, like Matty must feel. Assured. In control. As the rain began to fall faster, he and Alexandra rose – slowly, in spite of the advancing precipitation – and brought the laundry into the house.

Chapter 7

After Darnell and Alexandra had rescued the laundry from the rain, an awkward silence arose between them. What else could be said after what had transpired outdoors? The silence, uncomfortable though it was, nevertheless was unfortunately short-lived, broken by Lord Barnard's bellicose call.

"Darnell! Are you there?" he shouted from the top of the stairs. Darnell smiled a wordless goodbye to Alexandra, then turned swiftly towards his master's bellowing voice.

"I am, Lord Barnard. Would you care to see me?"

"Yes, of course, that is why I have called," he answered impatiently. "Please come up."

Left alone, Alexandra returned to her regretful reverie, now made more complex by Darnell's knowledge of her condition and his continued pursuit of her. She knew that as much as Matty desired her, he would never force her into something she did not want. This was comforting to her, and she committed to him the same easygoing manner in their public and private relations. And yet, in her current situation, it took more restraint on her part not to make Matty feel he must accept responsibility for the child she believed she was bearing – and to chain his own future to hers simply because this one time out of many their passion had apparently been productive.

Perhaps, she wondered, *it is wrong for me to be more concerned for his feelings than for my own health. After all, he is a man, he leaves his mark and withdraws and is unchanged. Yet I am a woman, and woman is vulnerable to all sorts of horrors and inconveniences that men know nothing about. That is how nature intended it to be, I suppose. And so I must be strong and bear this. And I can bear it. But to see cracks appear in Matty's confident and contented face is more than my heart can stand to witness. I must know more, ashamed as I am to admit it. For I know that Matty would not want me to care so deeply for him. And would he – could he – ever care so deeply about me?*

This was not a question she had about Darnell. If he was to be believed – and when couldn't Darnell be believed? – he was ready to commit his life to her, and to the baby as well. Darnell had soft hands. She wanted her baby's hands to be soft as well. It is well to work but hard manual labor is a station that is difficult to rise from. She wanted more for her child. Could Darnell provide that?

For his part, Darnell had taken the well-worn path up the stairs and into Lord Barnard's study. He smirked at the thought that he had been jealous of Matty and in competition with him for the attentions of both Lord Barnard and Alexandra. Matty's looks might open eyes and doors, but Darnell knew that he and he alone possessed the empathy, manners, and discretion that ultimately would prove him to be the more valuable to his master and the more attractive to his beloved Alexandra.

A test, he thought, *if only there were a test, a challenge I could accept that would prove to both Alexandra and Lord Barnard that I was the better man.*

Yes, if only. Yet even Darnell knew that though his thoughts were emboldened this day, he was as likely as not to shirk from such a trial should it ever be presented; at least, in the past this was so. Maybe he would indeed embrace a new chance to demonstrate the traits so deeply submerged in his personality that those who knew him best doubted they existed at all.

Such a challenge would have to wait, since Darnell's thoughts were struck dumb by the sight of Lord Barnard standing sourly behind his desk, on which lay a leather valise and an assortment of papers in and alongside it. He had clearly been rushing around to get ready for his trip, as the chaotic condition of the room was a far cry from the fastidiousness that was more typical of his peculiar nature.

"Yes, my Lord," Darrell said when he entered.

"Close the door," Lord Barnard ordered. "Darnell, I have an important assignment for you while I am gone."

"Of course, sir. Just tell me what you would have me do for you, and it shall be done."

"As you know, I am leaving tomorrow morning on a hunting trip," Lord Barnard started, all but clipping the end of Darnell's response. "I suspect that Lady Barnard will want to go to church on Easter Sunday. However, I have forbidden her to do so."

"Yes, I see," said Darnell softly.

"In spite of my orders, I have a sense that she will attempt to go anyway. If she does, if she leaves the house at all that day, I want you to come find our party and tell me. Our camp will not be far away; I specifically told Quentin that I wanted to stay near to town in the event I needed to hurry back. While it is my hope that she will obey my wishes, should she choose not to I want to be able to return quickly and catch her in the act of defiance. I will then deal with her as I must. Do you understand?"

"Y-Yes, my Lord," Darnell replied. "But how will I find you?"

"Here is a map that Quentin drew up. I know you are not a strong rider but even at a canter you should be able to reach us in an hour's time. The moment she walks out the door you are to seek us. If you don't tarry, we might succeed in returning home by the time church services have concluded."

"So, Lady Barnard is not to leave the house even to take fresh air, not even for a short spell?" Darnell asked.

"No!" shouted Lord Barnard. "I thought I made myself clear. She is not to leave the house at all. Not for a minute, not for a second. Not to attend church, nor to sit on the front steps. Now I ask again: do you understand?"

Hot blood rose to Darnell's face, though he was well-accustomed to modulating his voice in defiance of his inner feelings. Thus, though he felt a growing rage within, Darnell presented a calm exterior, saying simply, "I do." He took the map from Lord Barnard and walked from his office.

The bastard does not deserve the good woman who is his wife, he thought. And then he reflected on his use of the word "bastard." It was a slip of his mind's tongue, and he regretted it. He felt like a water bearer with a yoke on his shoulders: Alexandra and her unborn baby in one bucket, and the unfulfilled Lady Barnard in the other.

The sky outside darkened as the rain accelerated to a downpour and evening descended in kind. Lady Barnard, who earlier had heard the commotion yet not the content of her husband's shouting at Darnell, prepared pottage for dinner. This simple stew of cod, grains, onions, and turnips was well beneath them gastronomically. Minus the fish, it was what the poor people ate. (Had wild boar not recently become extinct in England, the forthcoming hunting trip might have yielded some of that tasty meat for a truly fine pottage.) Yet Lord Barnard preferred lighter meals and Lady Barnard had been raised on pottage and still enjoyed it. It was also easy to make and since the cook had been dismissed, ease trumped elegance.

The couple ate silently, the only sounds coming from Lord Barnard's impatient and overactive jaw. They drank wine, she three goblets to his one. After dinner, Lady Barnard summoned Darnell to clear the plates and invited him to help himself to a bowl of the pottage. Then the Barnards repaired to their separate rooms, leaving Darnell to wash the plates and put them away, after which he returned to his quarters.

Although there was excitement in the air throughout the village because of the approaching Easter holiday, the atmosphere within the house was stifling, as if it held too many people as opposed to two morose people. All lights had been snuffed by nine o'clock, except for a lamp in Lord Barnard's study, and his was the only body to remain in restless motion deep into the night.

In spite of retiring late, Lord Barnard woke early the next morning. He got his own breakfast of hard cheese, crusty bread, and strong coffee. He carried his valise and a satchel of clothing, no more than a day's worth. So sure was he that Lady Barnard would flout his authority, he did not plan to stay away a second evening. Furthermore, there was business to attend to with his solicitor this night, so there would be little time to crouch through brush and shoot at animals. His clothes, therefore, would not be too soiled in the event he was able to wear them again on this trip.

Matty had been alerted the previous evening to have the horses ready by daybreak. He was securing the bridles when Lord Barnard appeared at the stable door.

"Good morning, my son," said Lord Barnard.

"Good morning," a sleepy Matty replied.

"I expect to return from my trip with good news for you. And a new life for us both."

"Yes, my Lord," Matty said darkly.

"As much as I look forward to making you my heir, Matty, I will miss your expert hand with the horses. They look as ready for a parade as for an outing. You've done a wonderful job, as always."

"Thank you, my Lord," said Matty.

"You sound tired, my son," said Lord Barnard. "You have been working hard lately. I suggest you enjoy my time away by resting and celebrating the season. But do not indulge too heartily, for when I return you will spend many hours by my side, as there is much to teach you about being a gentleman."

And without a response from Matty, Lord Barnard took the reins of his brown mare, Kayleigh, and led her out of the stable. Shortly thereafter, Quentin arrived, along with Dennis Upham the tailor (a small man with a high forehead and bushy moustache) and Thomas Gallagher the banker (fat, as befits a man who counts other people's money). Quentin was too busy with his client and his party to speak with Matty, though he offered a wave to his friend, who looked on impassively from the stable door. Finally, Basil Finster, Lord Barnard's solicitor, arrived. Tall and serious-looking, with a permanently furrowed brow, he also carried a valise, and he and Lord Barnard conferred privately for a few minutes before joining the rest of the party and setting out on their trip.

"Are you able yet to talk about what's troubling you?" came a concerned voice from behind Matty.

Whirling around, Matty saw the familiar golden hair and inquisitive face of Alexandra. He smiled briefly, until he noticed the pale complexion of her sweet face.

"My troubles are my own matter," he said. "But what of you? Your face is white as bone. Are you not feeling well?"

"Bit of a sour stomach is all," she replied. "It happens. But you look to be of sour heart, which is most unusual for you. Come, Matty, what value is our friendship if you can only speak to me when you are gay? It has never bothered me that you share your bed with others, but I do not like it when you refuse to share your feelings with me. Have I not earned your trust?"

"Dear Alexandra," said Matty, taking her curls into his right hand, "I trust you as much as if you were my own blood. You are far too fine a friend – a lover – a woman – for the likes of me. I fear that the more you knew of me, and of what drives my desires, the less you would want ever to be with me."

"I care not about your past, Matty, and make no demands on your future," said Alexandra. "But I do want to know of today."

"All right," said Matty with trust in his heart yet resignation in his voice. "I shall tell you. But you must not repeat these words I tell you now."

"You have my vow," said Alexandra, her eyes wide and fixed in gaze at his.

Matty looked around to ensure they were standing a safe distance from Lord Barnard. He led Alexandra by the arm a few steps further along the side of the stable. In hushed tones, he spoke.

"Lord Barnard has plans to make me his legal heir," he said. "He will be making out the documents on this trip. When he returns, I shall essentially be his son."

Alexandra started to laugh, but Matty's expression told her that it was no joke – and his hand over her mouth reminded her that the subject of his secret was still on the property. Though Matty was known to tell tales, he could never make his audience believe something that wasn't true. In fact, as much as people enjoyed his stories, he loved them more himself. When he told a joke, his laugh was always the first and the heartiest. When spinning a yarn, his eyes and lips betrayed all the exaggeration of the narrative. Yet now, his stern expression made it clear to Alexandra that he was both serious and distraught.

"But what do you mean? How could this be?" she asked.

"The Lord is impatient at not having a child. You were right, I guess. It seems they don't bed together, and I'm not sure but I think it's because Lord Barnard is not right with women. So he wants to adopt me as his son and legal heir."

"Not right with women? What does that mean?"

"I don't know," Matty answered, "but I've heard from Quentin that he acts strangely. Looks at men quite a lot."

"Are you serious?" asked an incredulous Alexandra.

"Look, I told you I'm not sure of anything save for this: I do not wish to be his son," said Matty emphatically.

"Well, what will you do then?"

"I don't know," Matty replied, "and my dissatisfaction with my choices is what you have seen on my face lately."

"There certainly are advantages to being Lord Barnard's heir," said Alexandra, allowing herself to imagine a life with Matty as a man – and husband and father – of wealth and prestige. She realized this was unfair to Matty and unrealistic for herself, and so she quickly swept her statement out of the air where it had hovered between them with a new idea that was more sympathetic to Matty's plight. "Perhaps there is a way you can politely decline the offer?" she asked.

"If I do that, I'll tempt his ire and risk my job," said Matty. "And besides, who am I to disobey my master's wishes? He needs not my permission to make me his heir. I have no other family to claim me. He and his solicitor make it so, and it is so. The only option I've considered is to do some awful deed that would make it impossible for him to carry through his scheme. Something that would bring dishonor to him if we were to be legally bound together."

"Yet if that ploy was successful, you would have to leave here forever," said Alexandra. "Are you prepared to do so?"

"It would sadden me immeasurably, not least for the distance between us," replied Matty. "But then roving is not unknown to me, and I would rather live elsewhere as who I am than to remain here and be something that is disgusting to me."

"Then it seems you are decided after all, Matty," said Alexandra. "What will be the deed and when will it be done?"

"I have no answer for either question, but it must happen soon, before Lord Barnard returns," said Matty.

"Would you dare to do evil on Easter?" she asked.

Alexandra wanted to say more but she sensed a catch in her throat, and she was afraid of betraying her true feelings about the news. Matty perhaps sensed as much, yet with genuine feeling he again held her curls and said to her, bestowing a kiss on her clenched lips, "My dear Alexandra, with hair as fine as a bee's wings and the face of God's most favored angel, I would not go so far as the New World to escape Lord Barnard's wrath. He has not half my wiles, nor a tenth of my desire. I would find you and reunite with you under the shroud of darkness, no matter how many days I might need to travel to reach you. You will never be rid of me forever. And that is my promise."

With that, Matty kissed her again and Alexandra's heart filled. She did not doubt Matty's love for her in this moment. But could she trust it, come what may?

Chapter 8

Though neither could hear the exchange between Matty and Alexandra, both Lady Barnard and Darnell observed it, each staring out from a different window on the same wall and floor: Lady Barnard from her own room, and Darnell from Lord Barnard's study. In Darnell, the sight of the known lovers' earnest conversation, capped with a gentle kiss, produced anger; in Lady Barnard, who imagined herself in the place of the young and attractive Alexandra, the scene aroused passion.

For both lurkers, their visual eavesdropping served only to further enflame feelings they had already possessed. Darnell, still seething over Lord Barnard's cruel decree and incensed over Matty's lack of responsibility, felt protective of both Lady Barnard and Alexandra. Yet in truth, his attitude was not that of an altruistic benefactor, but rather of a frustrated suitor currently displaced in both instances by incumbents he loathed. To his chagrin, he knew that acting against either would be risky, and would not guarantee the ultimate objective he desired. Furthermore, Darnell was not a man of action. And so he reminded himself that patience would be required, for only if an opportunity for intervention presented itself – a test! – could he hope to advance his interests.

Lady Barnard, though flattered by Darnell's attentions, had not forgotten her first sight of Matty in the field. Rather than feeling jealous of Alexandra, the deserving wash girl confirmed Matty's aesthetic appeal and obvious virility. She began to feel a fluttering down below, her own imagination achieving more than her husband's fumbling hands were wont to do. She had Darnell to thank for opening her to the possibility that she could desire and be thought desirable. Yet the devoted assistant was not the one who could stoke her fire, who could strip away the years of unfulfillment and insert in its place a bounty of joy. She decided she must have Matty, even if it meant using her power and status in place of a more organic pheromone.

Darnell thought about Easter. He was to accompany Lady Barnard to church. To do so would be to conspire in defying Lord Barnard's orders. For both their sakes, he knew he should go to her and plead with her not to go to church tomorrow. But to please the master and thus displease the mistress struck him as foul, the exact opposite of what he desired to do. The alternative was to take her to church as planned, and then simply tell Lord Barnard that such never happened. The problem there was that Lord Barnard may have other spies in the village employed for the very purpose of catching them both in the willful act of non-compliance.

And if that be the case then so be it, Darnell thought with a bravado he could never speak. *What cad that would so seek to entrap his wife and loyal servant would be worth working for anyway?* Besides, he knew enough secrets that he could likely force Lord Barnard to maintain his employment for fear that he would tell all to the villagers.

Yes, Darnell in fact held something more powerful than mere position; he held knowledge, first-hand observations that he could use if need be to protect both his beloved Lady Barnard and his wages. They would go to church as planned, Lord Barnard be damned, and Darnell, the house servant who so often felt that the others envied and disliked him, who so long had been spurned by the object of his affection, he alone would have Lady Barnard's attention, if only for that one day.

Lady Barnard, too, thought about Easter. Surely this stable hand would go to church. All the servants would have the day free and she knew they enjoyed the chance to dress up and socialize among themselves.

I will go to church with Darnell, but I will make every effort to draw the attentions of this…this magnificent man, she thought. She quickly conceived a plan to meet and engage him: she would ask him to visit her that night and to guarantee his acceptance she would exert an influence she never had exploited before.

I will be bold yet confident. After all, I am a Lady and he but a keeper of horses. I could command him if he is at all hesitant about complying with my wishes.

And yet, once he came to her room that night, she knew it would be Matty who would have the power. She would willingly, most willingly, be submissive to his lead. He, after all, was the practiced lover, she the eager apprentice. Whatever his routine, whatever his rhythms, she would let him do to her what he does to Alexandra. He would direct her, tame her, mold her to his form and consume her, in ways she had never experienced before.

Intoxicated with her imaginings, she pulled herself away from the window and sat on her bed breathless.

Yes, she thought, *I will go to church in the morning and be saved in the evening.*

Darnell did not want to create a scene, here, the day before Easter, yet he felt compelled to interrupt Matty and Alexandra, if only to remind the latter that he was still a subject of interest, and the former that…well, that it is he who occupies a higher position and who therefore is due a level of deference. So he rather quickly descended the stairs, crossed the foyer, and stepped out the front door.

By this time, Lord Barnard and his hunting party had departed for the forest. Darnell crossed the yard and strode quickly to the stable. When he came upon them, Matty and Alexandra were no longer in embrace – and, in fact, were already moving apart from each other, he to the interior of the stable and she to the well.

However, while Darnell did not actually interrupt the two, his sudden bolting into view had the effect of startling the couple and drawing them nearer to each other in an instinctively defensive posture. He, in turn, was caught unawares when Matty, recovered from the momentary surprise, was the first to speak – and to speak in such a cordial tone.

"Darnell, my friend," Matty called out, "you've a well-deserved rest from the Lord's demands. This holiday is yours to enjoy."

"Er, yes, yes indeed," Darnell stammered. "Of course, there is the Lady to attend to. I don't know if you've heard, but I am to escort her to church tomorrow morning. Her desire to attend church is in conflict with

Lord Barnard's wishes so if you care for her well-being, you will not say a word about it."

"I am not one to gossip, Darnell, but I am certain that the two of you will make a lovely couple," said Alexandra in a friendly tease.

"I know so little about her, you know," said Matty, stepping nearer to the house servant. "She is quite shy, yes? Or maybe she prefers the indoors. I should like to hear more about her, and about the many important tasks you perform daily. We fieldworkers have no idea what it's like inside the house. What say you and I meet at the tavern tonight and talk over a few ales?" His strong hand now rested on Darnell's shoulder in a display of comradeship.

"What transpires inside the house, and especially with regard to Lord and Lady Barnard, is none of your concern," said Darnell with a slight tone of irritation. Matty touching him made him uncomfortable and Darnell's subtle shift of his shoulder failed to dislodge the stable hand's hand. Still, he was quite surprised and a little flattered at Matty's invitation. "It suffices to say that it is an honor to walk to Easter services with Lady Barnard on one's arm, wouldn't you say?"

"Oh, indeed," replied Matty, withdrawing his hand now, with Alexandra nodding in kind. "I envy and admire your position, which I can only imagine is one that is intensely challenging."

"Why yes, it is," said Darnell, pleased to have the fact acknowledged – all the more so coming from Matty. "You don't know the half of what I am asked to do."

"Truer words have never been spoken," said Matty. "And that is why I should like to learn more about it all. Come, it is the day before Easter, the master is away, it is time to relax and rejoice. The tavern-keeper owes me a few favors, we can drink on my account. What say you?"

Turning towards Alexandra, whom he hadn't paid attention to because he was fixated on Matty's surprisingly collegial overtures, Darnell asked, "Would you be accompanying us to the tavern as well?"

"A fine place that is for a woman," said Alexandra with a false tone of hurt that Darnell took as genuine. "What would the talk be about me were I to enter a house of liquor on the arms of two men?"

Darnell, embarrassed for suggesting that Alexandra place herself in a compromising situation only so that he would feel more comfortable accepting Matty's invitation, was about to bluster out an apology when Matty, with a hearty laugh, broke in, "What could be said about you, Alexandra, that has not been said before? Does not the fairest woman in the village deserve to be doted on by two reputable and debonair gentlemen? We three shall be the class of the tavern."

Now Matty embraced both Darnell and Alexandra about their shoulders, his muscular arms drawing them to his body. Darnell had never been this close to Matty before, and his rival's workmanlike aroma required his utmost discretionary powers to bear with a smile. Alexandra giggled, knowing how uncomfortable Darnell must be and marveling at his decorum.

And with that unifying declaration and gesture, the three figures agreed to meet back at the same spot at eight o'clock and walk together to the tavern.

As they went until then their separate ways, both Matty and Darnell were quite pleased: Darnell at the respect shown him and the fact that a popular man like Matty, rake though he was, had desired to include him in his revelry; and Matty because he had been successful in getting Darnell to drink with him. Once the effects of the alcohol began to play with Darnell's senses, Matty would ply him with questions about Lord Barnard's intentions. Maybe then Matty could gain some information that could be used against his employer and thus compel him to nullify whatever legal document his solicitor would soon be fashioning for him.

Perhaps he also would learn some things about the mysterious Lady Barnard.

As for Alexandra, she knew what Darnell did not: that Matty was playing him like a lute. At this she was not a little uncomfortable. Never before in matters involving the three of them had she ever felt a divided loyalty. While she did not feel a passion for Darnell as she did for Matty, he had established himself as a decent man who clearly cared for her, even in her current situation – a situation she did not feel she could so much as discuss with Matty.

I know that Matty intends to use Darnell for his own purposes, she reasoned, *but I do not fear that Darnell will come to harm. If I thought otherwise, I would not be able to accede to Matty's plan. In fact, my very presence may keep him from carrying the ruse too far, so I must participate. At the very least, I will have a chance to compare the two in a relaxed and neutral atmosphere. If nothing else, it will serve to take my mind off this pregnancy, which seems more certain with each passing day.*

Chapter 9

The area that Quentin had chosen for the hunting party's base camp was one he knew well. Though but a short ride due north from Lord Barnard's home, it was still largely virgin territory. Trails had been cut to reach a stream from which hunters and passers-by would let their dogs and horses drink. An associate of Lord Barnard's had been trying to convince him to invest in a mill to be built on the banks of the stream, but Lord Barnard was unconvinced the venture was sound. One would have to clear the entire forest and construct a village around the mill to house the workers, he argued, which would take too long to build and make it far longer still to recoup the costs.

Quentin had grown up about another ten miles northeast from there, and at age nine he and his family passed through the area on their way to the village to take up residence in his grandfather's house. His grandmother had died from influenza three months before, and the old man had proven incapable of caring for himself alone.

The "passing through" actually took three days, as Quentin's mother, pregnant to bursting at the time, began to have the child in the wagon just as it neared the stream. Quentin's father was a capable man and had delivered the last three of his four sons – the exception being Quentin, the oldest, who was delivered by an eccentric midwife who nearly threw the purplish squirming newborn into the basin because he was slow to draw his first breath.

Even so, Quentin's brothers had not developed quite as Quentin had and never seemed as bright, to the extent that some wondered if they might have fared better with the mad midwife. Whatever the truth, here in uninhabited territory there was no one else to whom they could turn. Quentin's father asked him to occupy his brothers in the woods while he attended to business in the wagon.

In the time it took for the sun to come from just above the treetops on one side of the sky to just above the horizon on the other side of the sky, Quentin and his brothers had run, skipped, climbed, hid, waded, dug, and rolled around nearly every square inch of land and water in the vicinity. Arriving back at the wagon as the dusk began to deepen, the boys were twice disappointed: first, to learn that they would not stay and live in these woods – though they had to stay put for a couple of days until Quentin's mother and the baby were strong enough to resume the journey – and second, that their newest sibling was a girl.

When, a couple of years later, Quentin was allowed to ride on his own, he began to return to the area to seek quiet relief from his chores. Still later, he would come to practice his marksmanship alone, as well as the challenging art of intimacy with girls whose layers of clothing seemed as dense as the woods themselves. He decided then that if he never was to live in these woods, he would like one day to die in them, to be buried beneath the moist soil of these sacred grounds.

Imagine, he wrote once in a letter to his father, *to be part of this rich forest floor, to decompose in this black earth, feeding the vegetation even at the expense of being fed upon by the bugs and worms who are fortunate enough to call this land their home. I would be among them and then forever I would abide in these woods.*

One night, several weeks after Matty had intervened in Quentin's fight with Phillip and his brother, during which interval Quentin and Matty had spent many a night at the tavern cementing their friendship with a mortar mixed of brown ale and barely exaggerated tales of their past, Quentin brought Matty to this place. There by the stream, they pledged brotherhood to each other. Quentin made a small gash in the meaty pad of his right thumb with a knife, then did the same to Matty's. They then shook hands, with thumbs erect so their blood could mingle. Finally, each licked the blended blood from his own thumb.

By this ritual, consecrated by the trees and witnessed by the owls and the ferns and the snakes, Matty had finally gained a brother, while Quentin had finally gained one his equal.

Now, to nearly the same location, Quentin had led Lord Barnard's party. Camp was set on a small flat hill; from this relative high ground, one could see and hear the stream they had crossed and which trawled along lazily not more than two hundred paces away. Spring had thickened the foliage, which limited visibility yet created a lush green backdrop that was both calming and quiet. Arms they had and sufficient in number to bring back as many kills as could fit in the wooden cart that Quentin's horse pulled along. As for the horses, they were tied to a tall oak tree, restricted to stare at its bark until they were loosened to visit the stream.

Yet hunting was not of primary interest for all this first day. Lord Barnard had sent Quentin to the stream to bring water for the camp, then instructed him to lead Upham and Gallagher out to find a deer or some rabbits for dinner. This he was happy to do, but Quentin asked Lord Barnard if he himself did not intend to hunt.

"Not today, Quentin," he said. "I have important business to conduct with Mr. Finster here. Hopefully we shall conclude by dinner. Tomorrow, I shall wish to remain near camp in case Darnell arrives with news. If he does not, then perhaps later in the day I shall try my luck."

Odd, thought Quentin. *Why come out to the woods to do business? Has the solicitor not an office? Is there something quite secret for them to discuss, something so private that they dare not do so in town lest someone should happen by the window and overhear?*

Well, it only served to confirm Quentin's idea of Lord Barnard that he was a strange duck. It was no matter to Quentin, after all. Here he was in his favorite location and if Lord Barnard would not point a rifle at prey, then that meant more shots for him. And so he took guns, powder, rope, and the tailor and banker, and walked deeper into the woods until to Lord Barnard and Finster they were no longer seen, and their footsteps – walking on last autumn's detritus of brown leaves and twigs – were no longer heard.

The solicitor and his client sat on a fallen oak, quite an old one judging by the generous seating space it provided, felled some time ago by what must have been a wicked storm. Finster spoke first.

"So then, Lord Barnard, what business have you that it must transpire here, apart and alone from our friends and townsfolk?"

"Do you know of Matthew Musgrave, whom I employ to tend my horses?" asked Lord Barnard.

"I've not met him," said Finster, "but tales of his exploits are many. I know no details of any in particular," he hastened to add. "After all, I'm not one to listen to gossip, least of all to the prurient kind, but in the cumulative, they have made his reputation secure."

"Exploits?" asked Lord Barnard. "Of what kind?"

"Well, surely you must know. After all, he all but lives under your roof."

"Are you suggesting that he is the carousing sort?" Lord Barnard inquired.

"My good friend," replied Finster, "Matty Musgrave has made the intimate acquaintance of nearly every maiden in our town, not to mention the surrounding villages. And more than a few matrons, if the chatter is accurate. I shall not say more, for I do not indulge in this sort of gossip."

"Well," said Lord Barnard after a short silence. Another short silence ensued, broken by a clearing of his throat, through which next came, "He is a handsome lad, to be sure. Young and full of strength and vigor. But how would you judge his character? As a person, that is. Would you say he is a good, honest fellow?"

"As I've said, I don't know the man personally," replied Finster. "I should think, however, that he might require some lessons and refinement if he were to be introduced to proper society as an honorable man. When the citizenry in the street speak of a person, it is either because he is respected or because he is a rogue. In the former instance, the talk serves to build the man's character and reputation beyond its current standing. In the latter, a low man is brought even lower, because he is known only for his misdeeds. I suspect that is the nature of the scuttlebutt of Mr. Musgrave. But why do we speak thus of your Lothario, Lord Barnard?"

"Finster, I think I know Matty better than most, and I can speak with authority that he is both wise and kind. I agree with you that he is not now ready to accept the mantel of 'gentleman', but with the proper tutelage I believe he can become a most respectable and influential man. You see, because my wife is barren, I need other means to gain an heir. I should therefore like to adopt Matty Musgrave as my own son and legal heir, effective immediately."

"Adopt Musgrave?" Finster asked incredulously. "Have you gone mad? You are a man of position. How would your reputation and honor endure such an arrangement? It's one thing to have him in your employ, after all no one expects a gentleman to clean an animal and shovel its dung. But to make him as your own son, why that's inviting derision upon your good name. I shan't be party to it."

Lord Barnard was unaccustomed to not getting his way, which informed the tenor of his response. "I asked you here, Finster, not for the words you would speak, which are too many, but the words you would write," he said. "You are to draft a document that fulfills my wishes and I expect you to do as I say, for if you refuse our professional association shall be forever terminated, *effective immediately.*"

And with that, Finster relented. Lord Barnard dictated the scope of what he desired in terms of his legal rights and the recognition of the town's governor that Matthew Barnard nee Musgrave was the son and sole legal heir of Lord and Lady Barnard. Finster asked questions, consulted a pair of legal tomes he had brought, and wrote out the document, the third draft of which Lord Barnard signed. Finster then affixed his signature as witness and executor, rolled and tied the document, and placed it within his bag.

This transpired as the day aged and darkened into dusk. In time, the hunting party returned. Quentin dragged a rope to which was tied two deer – one, a fine buck, he killed himself; the other, a faun, he had to put out of its misery as Upham the tailor's shot injured the young beast, yet not mortally. Gallagher the banker hit nothing but bark and earth. *Hands that count money are too soft and weak to make a good shot*, Quentin thought to himself on the walk back to camp. They feasted that night on the larger and older of the kills, and left the other in the cart to skin the following day.

All the while, back in town, Matty prepared for his night at the tavern with Alexandra and Darnell. He was unaware that he no longer belonged to himself, nor was the man he called himself. Though he had feared and may have suspected it, he could not have known that plans already had been made to relieve him of his duties attending to the horses upon his master's return, and that instead he would spend his hours in Lord Barnard's study, learning etiquette and matters of business, and leaving him little time and space free from the close gaze of his "father" with which to attend to the ladies of the town.

Yet as he changed into a clean shirt and smoothed his hair, his only thoughts were of what he could do to parry Lord Barnard's intentions. So preoccupied was he that he was startled back into the evening's plans only by Darnell shouting from outside.

"Musgrave! Are you joining us or have you a jug of your own by your wash basin?"

Matty took a few shillings from under his mattress and stuffed them into a small cloth pouch, which he then tucked into the waistband of his trousers. He called out as he walked towards the door, "Only the drunkard and the friendless drink alone." Joining Darnell and Alexandra in the road, he added, "Our party has convened. Let the merriment begin!"

So together, under a waxing moon climbing into a sky the dark green hue of ocean water, the three walked together to the tavern. Of the three, Matty was, not surprisingly, the most comfortable and confident. After all, he was in his natural element and had nothing either to prove or to hide. Darnell, on the other hand, felt alien and vulnerable in their company, like a ripe gooseberry in a bushel of hardy gourds. He did not trust Matty but did welcome the chance to spend an evening with Alexandra, fearing only that he wouldn't measure up against his rival's boundless charisma.

As for Alexandra, she was acutely aware that she and Darnell were in on a secret that Matty did not know, and worried that under the spell of alcohol the truth may come out. At the same time, she felt somewhat protective of Darnell because of the force of Matty's personality and the fact that she knew Matty sought to gain something from Darnell. Adding to these concerns, she did not feel well, had not much appetite, and tired more easily with each passing day. She intended to be more witness than participant in the frivolity and merriment sure to come.

The walk wasn't a long one but it was pleasant going, the calm elements of the day carrying over into evening, punctuated by a slight seasonal chill. Even before they were near enough to see the lamp lights emanating from the tavern windows, they heard the gaiety transpiring within. They spoke little to each other as they approached the building, but as he held open the door for his party, Matty quickly assumed the role of host. Thus, as the door closed behind him, Matty immediately raised his right arm and called for a round.

Chapter 10

"A holiday, and the first one of the year! Here's to the grandest of companions with whom to celebrate it." As he thus toasted, Matty raised his mug of ale, swinging it forward to clink against those held by Darnell and Alexandra with such gusto that rivulets of foam ran down the back and onto the arc between his thumb and forefinger. After taking a hearty swig, he slurped the bitter spill from his hand and laughed. "'Tis a shame that Lord Barnard is not present to have a drink with us, eh?"

"I shouldn't think he would share our table even if he weren't away hunting," said Alexandra, sipping from her mug, which contained a fermented cider known far to the south as scrumpy. "He's never been one to spend much time with the help – the two of you excepted, of course."

"Well, obviously, my position requires that I be in his company much of the time he is at home," Darnell was pleased to respond. "It is not often that he closes a door without permitting me to enter. Except," he tried not to frown, "except when he meets with you, Matty." At that, he gamely raised his glass, as if to compliment Matty on his own unique relationship with their employer. Taking the cue, Matty returned the gesture, and they drank again.

"As to your first statement, Alexandra," Darnell continued, "Lord Barnard is quite a sober man. Yes he takes the occasional drink, but never have I seen him do so to excess. So even if he were wont to pass the time with us in an informal setting, I doubt that the tavern would be his choice. Lady Barnard enjoys her wine – not in a bad way, mind you – but, of course, she is rarely permitted to venture far into town. I will thank you not to inquire as to why."

Devoid though it was of any trace of Lord or Lady Barnard, the tavern was a popular establishment this night. Even at an early hour, few were the jugs that held a cork for any length of time, and so the hops-scented air was thick with the festive din of hearty conversation, robust laughter, and unsolicited song.

Since his first day in town, when he wandered in and saved Quentin's life before even taking a drink, Matty had been a frequent visitor at the tavern. Which is not to say that he had a reputation as a drunkard because he did not. Truth to say, Matty was a frequent visitor to many places – save church – and was uniformly welcome wherever he went. Yet he did have a fondness for the tavern. He lived for companionship and made conversation easily with people of all stations, from the nobleman to the beggar. Further, given the smells with which he worked all day, he found the aroma of the tavern – an intoxicating concoction both yeasty and woody – a pleasing contrast.

The tavern was homey; in fact, it was the keeper's home. Informally (and secretly) for more than a year, Thomas Richardson had been brewing his own ale and charging visitors to drink it in his front room. For a few additional pence, he would play his fiddle for the patrons. Eventually, the authorities found out about his covert commercial enterprise and threatened to take his home unless he declared it a legitimate business and separated the serving area from his living quarters.

Richardson took a loan from the banker Gallagher and expanded his front room to comfortably accommodate as many as fifty people (though many nights, such as this one, half as many more were let inside). On the floor of wide wooden planks stood ten small tables, as well as counters built into the left- and right-facing walls. To the rear was the bar. On the other side of the wall behind the bar were the three rooms in which Richardson and his family lived.

Matty, Darnell, and Alexandra sat on high stools on the right side of the tavern, facing a window that looked out on the street. Matty was sure the venue was right for eliciting secrets from Darnell, but there had yet been sufficient time and liquor to loosen the house servant and cause him to speak with the freedom and frankness that Matty desired. Matty therefore playfully challenged Darnell to chug the remaining contents of their mugs, that they may be refilled with fresh brew. Uncertain, Darnell glanced at Alexandra, who smiled and nodded slightly. Though she knew she was abetting Matty's plan, she did truly believe that Darnell would benefit from being unguarded and relaxed this one evening.

With Alexandra's tacit approval, Darnell also believed that going along with Matty's sense of sport could only further endear himself to her. It was obvious that Matty and Alexandra were close; there was no benefit to being the odd man out. Having feared his ability to compare favorably with the stable hand, Darnell began to understand that Alexandra needed to see them together in order to realize more clearly what he offers that Matty does not. *She is not put off by the rascal in Matty*, he reasoned, *so I have license to be more assertive.*

"Not only do I accept your challenge," Darnell said at last, "but he who finishes last must pay for the next round." And then, when Darnell lost his own counter-challenge (as he knew he would; in fact, it took him a few seconds merely to catch his breath, find his voice, and wipe his chin), he said, "The penalty is mine, although I was set to procure the second round anyway since you bought the first." He raised his empty mug and waved it to catch Richardson's attention, and in short order a jug was brought to the table and the cups were refilled.

Darnell rose to inaugurate the second round with a toast. "I know my deportment is rather formal at times," he began. "It goes with the responsibility of my position, you understand. Yet while I am somewhat of a confidant of Lord Barnard's, I am not his colleague. I am *pleased* [such emphasis intentional to create the desired distance between himself and Lord Barnard] to mark this merry time with my fellow laborers, and may we enjoy many more such celebrations as this in the future."

Matty cheered heartily at Darnell's toast, not only for its literal sentiment but also because it was apparent that a single quaff had already loosened his inhibitions somewhat. Perhaps only two more and the information he sought would come dribbling out of Darnell's mouth like the saliva he'd spat when he uttered the word "pleased."

Alexandra was also heartened by the toast and by the fact that Darnell was indeed celebrating together with them. It was the first time the three of them had been together socially and she appreciated seeing Darnell in quite a different context. Darnell's reasoning was proving true and effective, as Alexandra was very much enjoying his company – not because he was acting like Matty, but because he was acting like a man. Neither a gentleman nor a ruffian, but a simple, normal man who can both work and play, each honorably.

She began to feel less like a co-conspirator, and was moved to offer her own toast.

"I should like to add my own salute, if I may," she declared, and her companions responded enthusiastically with shouts of "By all means" and "Hear, hear." Alexandra didn't stand, but she held her mug with an outstretched arm at chin level, directly between Matty and Darnell, so that to look at the mug they must necessarily see each other.

"We three toil for the same people," she continued, "yet our places and our histories are varied. Darnell, you have been here the longest. You work inside and it suits your sense of order and propriety. Matty, you have been here just longer than a year and you work out of doors with the horses, for walls and doors can never hold your spirit. As for me, I work inside when the weather is cold and outside when it is warm. I make things clean," she said with a self-deprecating laugh, "yet they always manage to get soiled again.

"I have been here a while and I have seen people come and go. There have been times I have felt lonely and misunderstood, and there have been times I have received wonderful kindnesses."

She looked back and forth at the two men.

"The work is not easy and it's never done for good. My place in life seems set, and I can't say truthfully that this is what I imagined for myself even a few short years ago. And yet, while there are difficulties that we all face, I sit here tonight before the Easter holiday, and I am with two friends who care about me. We can have fun and be silly, and leave our work behind. This feels good to me, and I wish it could continue forever. And so I say thank you to both of you, for being wonderful and for being together with me this evening."

Alexandra began to sip her cider when she noticed that neither Matty nor Darnell had moved or spoken a word both during and after her speech. Between the two, there was a blend of being touched by her words and yet also a slight discomfort at the intimacy she had described them sharing, when neither felt it quite true.

"Heavens, have I sobered us so soon?" she asked in genuine concern. Darnell and Matty then quickly recovered, for her sake if not for theirs, with a chorus of

"Amen" and "Well spoken." Matty clinked his mug against theirs and said, "We've just heard a lovely toast and so we must drink."

"Indeed," said Darnell, and then threw back his head and chugged the remains of his ale. "I've finished first this time," he said with unusual volume even given the setting, and Matty and Alexandra laughed gaily. When the next round was consumed, Matty decided it was time to begin fishing for useful information from Darnell's now-unguarded mind.

"I agree with Alexandra," said Matty. "I am most pleased that we all are here together. And I hope I'm not being too bold to suggest that I'm happiest yet for you, Darnell, for you seem to have less freedom to come and go as you would like."

"Yes, well, I'm often sent on errands, it's not as if I can never leave the house," replied Darnell. "But it's true that I am likely more constrained than the rest of the servants, by virtue of their need to have me close."

"And how do you like their company?" asked Matty, allowing nary a second to pass since the conclusion of Darnell's previous response.

"How do you mean?"

"Well, I'm sure the nature of your work is such that some of it is quite interesting, yet some of it must be pure drudgery. Seems to me that that's simply the nature of work itself. But apart from how you feel about the work you do for them, what is it like to be so frequently in the presence of Lord and Lady Barnard?"

"Come now, the experience is not unknown to you, Matty," said Darnell. "You've been in his office. He's come to visit you in the stable."

"Yes, true, of course, but I see him when he wants to see me," Matty replied. "He has a specific task or question for me and he gets right to the point, you know that about him better than anyone. Not one for idle chatter, right? But you, you see him in private moments, in rest and reverie. And the Lady, too, whom I see so rarely and know nothing about. How do you find them as people?"

"Well,…," Darnell started, then hesitated, as he was unsure of what to say or how best to say it (he was, after all, still a little more possessed of discretion than he was possessed by alcohol).

"Mind you," Matty assured him, "I'm not interested in gossip nor would I dream of asking you to reveal any secrets. You're far too honorable for that and I would never attempt to compromise your integrity. Here, let me fill your cup again, nice of old Richardson to leave the jug, easier than trying to get his attention each time, isn't it? It's just that you know them so much better than I do, and I'm curious, that's all."

Darnell took another drink. "Well, I don't mind sharing my impressions of them. On the whole, they are kind and fair. They both enjoy music – though neither play, which is a shame considering the exquisite spinet they own. I rather wish I could play, then I'm sure they would ask me to entertain them on it. Lord Barnard is an avid reader; you've seen the many volumes in his study, no doubt. I can vouch for the fact that he's read every one of them. They are even-tempered for the most part, she more than he. In fact, I'll never forget the first time I experienced – in fact, caused – his anger...."

Just then, Darnell's face broke into a crooked little smile as his eyes seemed to run inward, watching a scene being replayed in his mind.

"Wait, what is this?" asked Matty enthusiastically. Perhaps a nugget he could use. "Your face betrays a tale that must be told. Out with it."

"Yes, please," said Alexandra. "If you're comfortable, that is."

"Yes, it's fine. It's more about me than him, actually," said Darnell. "When I first began working in the house, I was often quite flustered. Lord Barnard was a bit more brusque in his demeanor than I had been accustomed to. When he wanted something, he wanted it without delay, and I was not always aware of where the thing was, or how to do what he asked. Well, he'd just come in from a hunting trip and I guess he had lost a wager with someone in his party and needed to quickly write a promissory note. He was not at all in fair spirits and as I followed him into his study he commanded me to get him a quill.

"Well, I knew where they were kept but the first one I picked up had a rather dull nib and I decided it wouldn't do. As I reached in for another one, Lord Barnard again demanded the quill. I was so anxious that I thrust it towards him point forward, and in the same moment he was darting his hand out to receive it. The point lodged itself rather deeply into his palm, the fleshy part below the thumb, actually, and he cried out in pain. Had I not run out of the room quickly to fetch a cloth, I fear he would have beaten me with his riding crop."

Matty and Alexandra both laughed at the tale, Matty less heartily because it provided no clues as to what he should do about his own matter with Lord Barnard. But

Darnell enjoyed the story as well, and was pleased to be regarded as so jolly by his two colleagues. He therefore drank all the more heartily, finishing the portion that Matty had drawn for him, and calling for more.

"I wonder," said Matty, "if Lord Barnard carries a scar on that hand to this day."

"He does," answered Darnell, "for that quill had been used once that day already and the ink that remained on the nib lodged under his skin. He bears a small black 'v' on his right hand. It's small all right, but plain to see if you know to look for it."

"How remarkable," said Alexandra. "I imagine Lady Barnard must have been alarmed by the racket."

"Indeed she was," said Darnell. "When I returned, she was there dabbing the wound with a cloth soaked with spirits. Lord Barnard was protesting that it worsened the pain, but she continued to tend to him as I looked on. Rather sheepishly, I must add."

"Is she handy with cures, then?" asked Alexandra.

Darnell paused, then sighed before responding, not actually addressing her question directly. "Lady Barnard is caring and kind as an angel," he said at last, in tones both of admiration and regret. "I wonder sometimes if Lord Barnard appreciates her qualities as he should. I mean, the very fact that he does not allow her to venture into the village at all. I mean, really. Why, if he even knew that I was escorting her to church tomorrow he would be blind with rage."

"Is that so?" said Matty, becoming quite interested in Darnell's testimony. It was obvious to both Matty and Alexandra that Darnell seemed protective of Lady Barnard. "Please do tell us more. She sounds like such a lovely woman, but how sad that she is kept like a caged bird by Lord Barnard. I envy that you know her so well. I'm not sure she even knows my name. I've never once seen her at the stable."

"She is fair, indeed," said Darnell. "Fairer yet when she smiles, which is all too rare, I regret to say." He paused. "Yes, serving Lord Barnard is my duty," he continued at last, "yet serving Lady Barnard is my pleasure."

"So much so that you risk Lord Barnard's wrath?" asked Matty.

"Without hesitation," replied Darnell.

"Tell me, then," said Matty, "what exactly do you think Lord Barnard would do if he found out you took her to church? And mind you, no word of this shall pass my lips while there is breath in my body."

"I imagine I would be fired and banished," said Darnell. "He would insist that I never pass before or onto his property for as long as we both shall live. And that would be fine with me."

This last remark surprised both Matty and Alexandra, yet they were unable to ask for further clarification because just as he finished his sentence, Darnell's head fell forward onto the table. Matty's plan had worked perfectly: Darnell became more talkative as he became more inebriated, he unwittingly gave Matty the information he was seeking, and he would remember almost nothing of the evening when he awoke the next morning.

Matty and Alexandra arose, and Matty lifted the sleeping servant onto his shoulder. With his free hand, Matty tossed a few coins on the counter, and he and Alexandra walked back to the Barnard residence. In a few hours, the church bells would ring and none of the townspeople's cumulative joy would equal the pain and agony that the reverberations would cause Darnell as they clanged and echoed in his aching head.

Chapter 11

It was an unusually quiet morning in the house when Lady Barnard slowly stirred herself awake. The rising sun, throwing its orange darts of light low across the village, was not blocked but rather recast in hue as it shot through her collection of colored glass that sat on the shelf by her windowsill, creating a kaleidoscope of bright, warm splotches on her still-drowsy face.

On a more typical day, the sound of Lord Barnard, ever an early riser, walking through a succession of rooms to find an item misplaced – a book, often; sometimes a letter or an article of clothing – would begin to rouse her. His inevitable call to Darnell to help with the search or to prepare his papers for work, and the loyal servant's prompt response, would complete the process of her awakening.

This morning, however, she rose on her own, as her husband was off in the woods and Darnell was still in the hold of a heavily liquored sleep. She sat up slowly in her bed, looked around with a questioning expression on her face, then became energized with the dawning realization that it was Easter Sunday, that she would be going into town, accompanied by Darnell – yet looking out for the handsome, virile stable hand.

Lady Barnard pulled back the quilt and swung her legs over the side of her bed. The silence in the house did not bother her, nor did the fact that she was alone.

It is worse to feel alone when you are in the company of others, she often thought, *than when you are, in fact, alone*.

Lord Barnard had once offered to hire her a servant of her own, a girl to help bathe and dress her, mend her clothes and make curtains, and any other tasks Lady Barnard may desire. Yet she would have none of it. She was too modest to allow a strange person to have such intimate contact with her, and she preferred to do her own sewing, one of the first skills she was taught. The wash girl Alexandra was sufficient for tending to the remaining textile requirements.

She was glad she had no servant like Darnell – who, though he willingly served her, was clearly and primarily beholden to Lord Barnard – scurrying about her personal space all day looking to please her in myriad ways that were most unpleasing to her.

Luxuriating this morning in her temporary solitude, and truly inspired by the thoughts of what this day might bring, she removed her nightgown and strode nude to the wash table on the far side of her room. Separated from the rest of the room by a hand-painted screen given to her by a cousin of Lord Barnard's – which he'd acquired on a business trip to the trading port of Macao, the peninsula off the southeastern coast of China that the Portuguese had settled a century before – the wash table held on its marble top a large blue and white porcelain basin filled the previous afternoon by Alexandra with fresh well water. A looking glass was suspended from a hook on the wall behind it. A cake of scented soap lay waiting on a small silver dish to the right. A folded towel sat to the left. Atop the towel was a sponge.

Lady Barnard wetted the sponge in the basin water, then rubbed it against the cake of soap. She applied the foamy mass first to her shoulders. Streams of water ran down her collarbone and blazed a trail across her breast. She noticed the instant eruptions of goose pimples on her skin, dwarfed by the involuntary extension of her nipples. She was beginning to understand that her body was a living thing, that it responded naturally to certain stimuli. Touch, temperature, even thoughts created changes.

As much as Lady Barnard had suffered emotionally from a lack of interaction with people in the village, her body also suffered from its isolation, like a discarded dulcimer with unstruck strings or an indigestible bread made from dough insufficiently kneaded.

She wanted to bathe slowly, to revel in her awakening acknowledgement of her body's form and feeling, yet she also was impatient to get dressed and leave the house. She recalled the previous two Easters, when Lord Barnard grudgingly would escort her to church. It was apparent that people lingered in the street before and after the service, so as to see each other and make plans to celebrate the day together. Yet she had not been party to this social practice, as Lord Barnard made a point of arriving to the church just as Rev. Collins was closing the door, and heading straight back to the house as soon as the last refrain of the closing hymn was concluded.

Today, she hoped, would be different. She would arrive early, remain late, see and be seen, admire and be admired.

And so she bathed the rest of her body more rapidly, rinsed with the bracing fresh water, and toweled herself dry. She then opened the front door of the wash table and pulled out a rectangular wooden box that had been stained the deep brown color of a dark bay mare. Lined with crimson silk, it held her collection of scented powders and oils. The box had been untouched since last

Easter, as she had long abandoned the notion that it mattered how she presented herself to a public she would never see. She applied powder to her face and oil behind her ears, within her cleavage, and, playfully, on her thighs and buttocks.

She dressed in equal haste, pulling on the frilly yellow vestment with decorative buttons made of ivory and a white lace trim to match that sewn onto the bonnet she'd commissioned, which had been delivered the day before by Mr. McDougall. He was very pleased with his creation, and Lady Barnard complimented him on it with great sincerity.

Of course, she did not have access to her husband's funds, nor could she ask him to pay for it, for she was not supposed to be going out this day and therefore should have no need for such a fine new bonnet. Instead, she offered Mr. McDougall a ring given to her by Lord Barnard on their intensely awkward first meeting, which she had always worn on her right hand. It was a simple band of pewter he had made himself – with his father's extensive help and persistent encouragement – but over the years it had become too tight on her finger and the constriction hurt her. She would be glad to be rid of it, and if Lord Barnard were to notice she would say it had fallen off while bathing and became lost beneath the floorboards.

McDougall accepted it with gratitude, and with the vow that he would not show or speak of it to anyone in public.

Now bathed, powdered, and dressed, Lady Barnard prepared to summon Darnell. His room was a small, low-ceilinged space in the basement, an area of the house she was not wont to enter. Yet with Lord Barnard not at home and none of the other servants working (due to the holiday, of course), she was forced to step gently down the cellar stairs (so as not to soil her clothing) and knock upon his door.

It was the third of an increasingly forceful series of three raps that produced the sound of movement from the other side of the pine door. Darnell, still in the clothes he wore to the tavern the night before, began to stir during the second series. At the end of the third series, he began steadily to realize his state, his location, and, by dint of the light he could see out of the narrow pane high in the wall that provided his only view to the world outside, the approximate age of the morning. The time obviously being late, Darnell thrust himself out of bed in a panic, his boot catching the blanket and causing him to tumble onto the floor – this the sound that Lady Barnard heard.

"Darnell, are you all right?" she called. "Are you ready?"

His head heavy and aflame, Darnell began a desperate dance of undressing, washing, and redressing, hoping to accomplish in seconds what he had planned to spend half of an hour doing earlier in the morning.

"My apologies, Lady Barnard," replied Darnell while throwing hand-wells of water onto his face. "I require just a few minutes more, if that's all right. I shall come up to get you the very second I am ready. I most deeply regret my delay."

"That's quite all right, Darnell," Lady Barnard lied. "I shall await you upstairs." With that, she turned to ascend the stairs, her earlier excitement giving way to anxiety at the prospect of missing anything.

For Darnell's part, there was only anxiety. He had but faint memories of the night before, none between Alexandra's toast and his waking abruptly to Lady Barnard's knocking. He was unconscious when Matty and Alexandra walked him home, his ale-logged body slung over his rival's shoulder. When they arrived at the house, Alexandra opened the cellar door from which Darnell could come and go in his private hours without passing through the common areas of the house. Matty crouched through the opening so his burden would not strike against the frame. He dropped Darnell rather unceremoniously onto the bed and turned to leave. With hand gestures, Alexandra instructed Matty to go back and place the blanket over Darnell's body. He did so, then left Darnell to his drunken dreams.

Outside the house, Matty had invited Alexandra to spend the night in his loft in the stable. She politely declined, citing the lateness of the hour and her wish to rise early to prepare for Easter. So he walked her back to her cousin's house, then returned to the Barnard estate and went into his room in back of the stable. Matty slept well and rose early, taking a bathing swim in the pond behind the stable, where the horses would often take their drink.

The crisp, cool water refreshed and invigorated his naked body, and he eagerly awaited the festivities of the day and the opportunity to enact his plan – one that he was sure would guarantee his freedom and independence from Lord Barnard. His only regret was not to have had a final coupling with Alexandra, for he was sure that he would have to leave for new environs once Lord Barnard found out what he had done.

Maybe, he thought, *I could try to live alone in that wooded area that Quentin favors so well. There was space and wood enough to build a fine little cabin, and a stream for drinking, cooking, and bathing. Maybe I could even ask Alexandra to go with me.*

As for that wooded area, it still was occupied by Lord Barnard and his party. All arose early that morning, none earlier than Lord Barnard himself. He was up before the sun and had to add desiccated branches and deep breaths to the gray, smoldering embers of the previous night's campfire in order that he could read by the flickering yellow light of the resuscitated blaze. As the sun began its slow, steady ascent from beneath the verdant horizon, the rest of the party awoke on their high ground to a spectacular panoramic view of the transitioning skyscape, with pink and orange hues in the east and violet and cobalt in the west.

Quentin took advantage of the fire to heat water for coffee. There was some deer meat left over from the previous night's feast, but the consensus was that a fresh woodland hare or two would make a more satisfying breakfast. Quentin offered to hunt them alone – preferred to, in fact – yet Lord Barnard, not having joined the hunt the day before and awake nearly three hours already, was keen to join him. And so while the rest of the party moved leisurely through their morning paces, Quentin and Lord Barnard took up arms and went after the small game.

The two walked in silence until they were well out of sight from the camp. This was necessary in order to hear the cautious footsteps of the forest's little creatures. Yet the quiet was also a consequence of the two men's differing attitudes towards the other.

For Quentin, he was here with Lord Barnard for purely practical reasons: he was hired to lead the party and would be paid well for his efforts. He had proven his worth over a number of excursions and though he disliked and mistrusted his patron, for matters both of pride and of necessity he was committed to continuing to earn Lord Barnard's favor. His lack of speech, therefore, was due to his focus on successfully shooting breakfast – or aiding Lord Barnard in doing so – as well as his disinclination to speak to him beyond the necessities of his role.

As for Lord Barnard, he was thinking less about firing at a rabbit or raccoon than he was about the paperwork he had completed the day before. Even he had to admit it was queer that a man's status as a person should be altered so drastically with just a sheet of paper strewn with legal jargon and made binding by two signatures rendered with quill and ink. Furthermore, the person in question was neither present nor definitively aware of when and where the course of his life had irrevocably altered. No one else in the hunting party had knowledge of what Lord Barnard and Finster had conspired to do.

This, too, gnawed at Lord Barnard. He wanted to share his news but felt that apart from he and his solicitor, Matty should be the next informed. Yet he wasn't here and the knowledge was ready to burst out of Lord Barnard's mouth like a shot from a rifle.

As they slowly walked and gently stepped, Lord Barnard's mind raced and pounded with the need to divulge his secret. And here he was with a young man he both liked and trusted. He weighed the consequences of breaking their silence, knowing full well that Quentin and Matty were friends. Yet Lord Barnard was of the mind that Quentin would be happy both for his patron and his chum, and certainly he could buy the skilled hunter's silence with a bonus pouch of shillings. At any rate, he intended to cut the hunting trip short and return at first light the following day in order to begin remolding Matty's life from stable boy to gentleman as quickly as possible.

And so it was Lord Barnard who first broke the silence, his outburst so sudden that Quentin heard three sets of scampering footsteps race away before he even understood what Lord Barnard was saying.

"Quentin, I have the most marvelous news to share and I simply cannot maintain my peace a moment longer," he said, as Quentin's eyes darted about to watch the trails of brush movements indicating where the game had gone. "I beg your attention for this concerns our mutual friend, Matty."

At the mention of Matty's name, Quentin's attention focused more clearly on Lord Barnard, and he looked at him quizzically.

"I have not known Matty nearly as long as you have," Lord Barnard continued, "yet I dare say I am as fond of him as are you. Though some think of him as something of a rogue, I see in him a rough jewel who is merely in need of refinement. I can help him to fulfill his potential as a gentleman, and so have worked it out with my solicitor to adopt Matty as my own son and sole heir. He is, for all legal purposes, Matthew Barnard even as we speak."

Quentin's mouth opened yet he did not betray the silence he had kept. Then his mouth closed and he looked down, as if something had literally fallen from his lips.

"Well, have you nothing to say about this?" asked Lord Barnard, impatient for a response after Quentin's pause. "Certainly you are surprised, who wouldn't be? But are you as excited for your friend as I am for both him and for me?"

Despite an additional few seconds of muteness, Quentin did finally find his tongue. "I-Is Matty aware of this? Has he given consent to be…adopted?"

The question displeased Lord Barnard. Aside from snuffing his excitement, it was an unnecessary query and avoided the question of whether Quentin approved. "If you must know," he said somewhat sternly, "I did speak to Matthew about this matter, however I did not ask his permission because I do not require his permission. He is not attached to family, nor has he anything – whether food, shelter, or clothing – that is not due to my generosity. I all but own his life and livelihood already. What is new is that he has my name as of today, and in the future will have my fortune as well. I should think any man would envy him."

"Oh, quite," said Quentin, realizing he was at risk of falling into disfavor with Lord Barnard. "In fact, my joy for Matty is rivaled only by my…uh, envy of him. I merely wanted to know if he might be celebrating his good luck even as we speak."

"He will know for sure when we return to the village. At that time, I will tell him myself and make suitable quarters for him in the house. Now listen well, Quentin," Lord Barnard continued. "You are a man in whom I have placed my faith, and a large number of silver coins, many times. Never have you disappointed me. No one save you, Finster, and I know this information. No one else will know it until Matthew knows it, and only I will speak to him about this. Do you understand, and do you agree to utter not one word of this to anyone until I have done so first?"

Immediately upon uttering this last question, Lord Barnard placed a bag of coins in Quentin's hand. Quentin knew this represented a bonus – and a bribe. He did not know what ultimately he would do, but at this moment he had no choice but to accept it. "I do, Lord Barnard," he said, as his fingers closed slowly around the leather pouch. "I do."

Lord Barnard smiled. "I shall be looking for a new man to care for my horses," he said. "I would greatly value your opinion should you know a suitable candidate." Just then, a hare darted out from behind a towering maple. Lord Barnard lifted his rifle and took aim. He fired once and the hare fell back. Lying still, with a trail of scarlet spilling onto its fair auburn coat of fur, was breakfast.

Chapter 12

Alexandra awoke in her cousin's house Easter morning with a stomach complaint akin to what Darnell felt. Yet while Darnell's condition was rare and acute, for Alexandra the experience was by now familiar and indicative of a longer-term condition. The conclusion was inescapable: she was pregnant. How far into her term she could not be sure; a month perhaps, maybe as much as a fortnight beyond that. She had no way to know for certain.

Of her condition, even when it was merely presumed and not known to be fact, Alexandra had been concerned and nervous, yet never upset or regretful. She'd never thought about bearing children, yet it was not something she very well knew how to avoid. She wished for luck and for years had been granted such. When finally it seemed that the curse of barrenness was not to be her fate, she accepted it, unashamed of her circumstance. Her only worries were about Matty: how would he respond to the news, would he maintain his affection for her, would he bear responsibility for the child?

This day, it being Easter morning, the concept of new life took on a deeper layer of meaning for Alexandra. She allowed herself to think well beyond matters of patrilineage and the immediate consequences of her situation, and to fantasize about what kind of a person this child would become. Male or female, no offspring of Matty Musgrave could help but inherit his compelling physicality, his unforced nonchalance, and his adventurous and playful spirit. Surely some of the rougher edges and wilder inclinations would be tempered by her own maternal influence, but one would never doubt, regardless of whether Matty admitted it or not – or was present in their lives or not – that he indeed was the father.

(The wonder, frankly, is how there could not have been scads of easily identifiable little Mattys scurrying about and making mischief in the streets of the villages he'd called home.)

What, then, would that mean for Alexandra should Matty abandon her and refuse to claim the child as his own? If, say, she accepted Darnell's proposition? Despite the previous night's drunken frolic, she knew he still detested Matty – would so even more given the unceremonious end of the evening and what she assumed was already an unsatisfactory start to his day. Would he, therefore, also detest Matty's child? Could he ever look upon the child not as Matty's but as his own, in not only a legal but also an emotional manner? Or would Darnell use his promise to compassionately father the child merely to win her hand?

Then, of course, there was the added intrigue due to Matty's impending new status. *Surely*, she had allowed herself to imagine, *as heir to Lord Barnard he would enjoy a comfortable life and would be able to give the same to his wife and child.* Alexandra also understood that his days as a lothario would be ended, as his "father" would never permit him to indulge in such behavior.

Although, she realized, *it is unlikely that Lord Barnard would approve of his son marrying a wash girl and acknowledging a child conceived prior to taking the vows of matrimony.* Indeed, it seemed unlikely she would ever be in line for an inheritance that would improve her station.

That knowledge served to sway her private deliberations back towards Darnell as being perhaps the best choice of husband and father. And yet – how confusing it all was! – Alexandra could barely imagine the reality of Matty commanding not only the man who would raise his child, but also the woman who carried it.

A large house indeed is Lord Barnard's, she pondered, *but can it accommodate Matty, Darnell, me, and a child sired by Matty who would possibly know only Darnell as its father?*

     The complexities of her situation were far too much to contemplate on a day such as today. Desiring not to be late to church, and curious to see how the players in her intricate and intimate dilemma would behave the night after – *did Matty get the information he sought, has he a plan, and if so when will he enact it?* – she quickly bathed and dressed in a loose-fitting gown, and headed out the door for the short walk to the church.

     By this time, of course, Darnell had thrown himself together and run hastily up the stairs to Lady Barnard's quarters. His boots he held in his hands as he ascended the staircase, bending over to pull them onto his feet only after knocking on her door. And that is how Lady Barnard found him when she opened it. Sheepishly looking up at her with purple-lidded bloodshot eyes, he apologized a second time – this one he'd taken a few harried moments to prepare, knowing he would have her ire to soften.

     "My Lady, I do deeply regret my delay this morning," Darnell uttered quickly from memory. "Not the least because I have missed several moments when I could have beheld your radiant loveliness. Forgive me if I speak inappropriately, but never before in my years of service to you have I seen you more captivating. Surely no angel attending to our risen Saviour is as exquisite."

Though blatant flattery, Darnell's words did have their intended effect, as Lady Barnard's expression relaxed into a smile. She was well-pleased that he found her attractive, though her ambitions this day went beyond the dutiful praises of the house servant. She wanted – needed – the attentions of, to her mind, *a man who knew about lovemaking; a man who had sampled widely and would show me why the wash girl should smile so sweetly when he pays her a visit.* That man was the stable hand, whom she still did not know by name. Yet soon that would change. Lady Barnard would see to that.

"Thank you, Darnell," she replied to him. "Now you are ready and so handsome, let us make haste for church."

They descended the stairs, he on her right, holding her hand at shoulder level to steady her while she used her left hand to hold up the bottom of her dress. For Darnell, despite the throbbing pain in his head, this was a moment of courage and triumph. The former, because of what he risked in defying Lord Barnard's explicit orders. The latter, because the oft-ridiculed house servant, so long emasculated by the unfair comparison to his Adonisian rival, had now the most coveted lady in Lancashire county on his hand and by his side on this most special of days.

As soon as they reached the front porch, Lady Barnard could see the citizenry gathering in the street. She was eager to join them and all but pulled Darnell down the front steps with her. As they walked into town, Lady Barnard was entranced by the sight of so many people arrayed in their finery – or what passed for it, as few had the means to bedeck themselves in the elegant fabrics and jewels she had donned – and talking and laughing gaily in the morning sun.

They seemed to her like a bouquet of butterflies flitting and fluttering about. And when she passed through a throng, they scattered aside, not only in respect to her ladyship, but also in awe of her clothing and overall appearance. It reminded her of how she would run through a flock of birds as a child and delight in how they would flee from her waving arms and stomping feet, then she would beckon them back to her by spreading handfuls of her father's grain on the ground.

This was what she had yearned for and needed. She was among the people, she had their attention, and they were both pleasantly surprised and soundly impressed by her beauty. Of course, this satisfied Darnell's wishes as well, and in spite of the pain and nausea that wracked his insides he held his chin high with rare feelings of pride and self-satisfaction.

For Lady Barnard, however, this was just the beginning of satisfaction. Her true desire was not to be above the crowd – separate from it, as she had been before – but truly to be part of it. And so she tried, a bit awkwardly at first, to converse with them, to wish them a good holiday, to compliment the better of the bonnets and dresses that she saw.

The result was more than she could have anticipated. The townspeople, sufficiently delighted at merely the rare sighting of her, were positively entranced to learn that she was open, kind, and curious. More of them crowded around her, slowing her progress to the church. Not a few noted that her demeanor, so different from past years, was all the more engaging now without the presence of her husband, a man many respected but for whom few felt affection – or even really knew. Their indifference to him had never quite been directed with the same fervor at Lady Barnard, partly out of pity for her, partly because not enough was known of her to form an opinion.

In truth, no one in the town had much direct contact with her, if any at all. The man on her arm this day, Darnell the house servant, was for all intents and purposes her agent in the village. He ran almost all of her errands, and communicated her requests to various vendors. The people did not think much of the fact that Darnell was her escort to church – most knew Lord Barnard was out of town (though none knew he had prohibited his wife from leaving the house) and, after all, a servant does what a servant is commanded to do – though Darnell imagined that his stock among the people with whom he dealt daily rose significantly by virtue of his being seen with her in public.

Though she was impatient to actually get to the church for Easter Mass, she was only too happy to indulge her newfound admirers and she radiated pure pleasure at their close company. Darnell, however, took it as his responsibility to ensure that the presumed objective was achieved, and begged the crowd to move along so that all may begin the holiday commemoration. Thus, their pace accelerated, and soon the church, from steeple to steps, rose into view.

The church was set up on an elevation flanked by a dense grove of pine trees. The ornate mahogany doors and stained glass windows were imported from Italy (through connections of Lord Barnard's father, who also contributed a significant share of their cost), but the parishioners were proud to have done most of the construction themselves. The elder Barnard, in fact, had fashioned a number of the pews himself using the adjacent supply of pine.

The front lawn of the church was of a sufficiently low grade that it was easy to walk up to the entrance from the street. Lush green and clear of the towering trees that brought shade to the other sides of the structure, the grounds were a popular site for picnics and games. And if Reverend Collins noticed that there were more than a few who came often for recreation and rarely or never for spiritual reflection, he was heartened that they at least had come to pass their time on sacred ground.

When Darnell and Lady Barnard entered the church, they continued to attract the stares of the congregation. Swiftly, they walked towards the front pew. As they approached it, a man sitting on the end arose and offered the lady and her escort his seat. It was Matty, and he smiled and bowed at Lady Barnard with his most affecting expression. Her heart fell out of its rhythm momentarily and she nearly gasped at finally seeing from less than an arm's length away the man about whom she had fantasized. Recovering her composure, she nodded to Matty and proceeded forward into the pew. Darnell, at her side, came after, greeting Matty with a thinly veiled sneer.

When was the last time Matty came to church on time, he wondered, *and when had he ever sat so close to the Virgin (or any virgin)?*

Indeed, having sacrificed his seat, Matty moved to the rear of the church. Lady Barnard turned to watch him walk away. Without removing her eyes from his departing backside, she leaned towards Darnell and inquired, "What is that man's name?"

"That is Matthew Musgrave, who minds Lord Barnard's horses," he replied, not without a trace of derision in his voice. "He is called Matty. I hope he has not tracked in straw that may soil your clothing."

Lady Barnard nodded with a wisp of a smile upon her lips. She might have turned back to steal another look at the object of her longing, but the choir launched into a hymn she only faintly heard as her attention turned inward to the theatre of her imagination, where the curtains were slowly opening.

Darnell looked around, saw Alexandra sitting off to the side, slightly apart from the others in her pew. *At least she is not sitting with Matty,* he thought. He had the sensation, real or imagined he couldn't tell, of Matty staring at him from the rear of the church.

Darnell wished he could remember more of what transpired the night before, particularly what he might have said while intoxicated. He suddenly felt very vulnerable and thought it ironic that he seemed to feel so much more secure on the street than he did here in church.

Chapter 13

Unbeknownst to both Darnell and Lady Barnard, Matty had left the church after giving up his seat. He intended all along to make her acquaintance before the service commenced, and in fact had grown concerned that they were late in arriving. He was afraid both that he would miss his opportunity to make her introduction, and that he would be forced to endure the entire service from the front pew.

Fortunately, they arrived in time for him to make a quick impression and exit. He acknowledged, as he stepped aimlessly about the green lawn outside the church, that it likely was his fault they were tardy. Surely Darnell could have used a full day of rest after his rare evening of revelry. Matty smiled at the picture in his mind of Darnell, intoxicated to the point of unconsciousness, being flung onto his bed like a sack of soiled laundry.

He was pleased that his plan thus far was working perfectly. The first point had been accomplished last night: he realized how best to betray Lord Barnard. The second, getting the attention of Lady Barnard, was just realized. The third had to wait for the conclusion of the church service. He would be sure to stand in the open, so that when Lady Barnard walked out she would find him easily.

As he stood looking at the door of the church, he was surprised to see it suddenly swing open. The service surely would not end until the sun was directly overhead. Indeed, it was not the entire congregation leaving the church, but just one person. It was Alexandra, her head down, her step brisk – though seemingly in discomfort rather than in simple haste.

"Ho there," Matty called out, not too loudly. Alexandra stopped and looked up. She was not pleased to be spied, as she tried to leave discreetly, but was relieved that it was only Matty. Still, she was not in a mood to speak. The service had made her surprisingly emotional, and she felt somehow exposed sitting among the townspeople. She wished to be alone until this sensitivity, this fragility, had lapsed.

"Oh, hello, Matty," she replied gamely. "How odd to find you not in church."

"Quite odder to see you sneak out of it early, Alexandra," he replied. "Are you not well?"

"Just a bit uncomfortable, that's all. Thought the fresh air would revive me."

"I hope it does," said Matty. "But as you have previously suggested to me, sometimes speech also can cure ills. You have been ailing for some time now, yet you have never revealed to me what is the cause."

"In due time, my dear," Alexandra replied. "I promise you that I have no fatal affliction. All I require is some rest." She turned to walk away but Matty continued to engage her.

"Have I done something wrong to you, Alexandra?"

She stopped and smiled wistfully. "No, dear Matty. You have never done anything to me that I did not desire you to do. There will be a time, soon, when I will tell you what is going on with me. At that time, all I'll need from you is the affection and the respect you have always shown me. But for now, I simply need to rest."

With that, she reached up to kiss his cheek, then they embraced. As Alexandra turned and walked away, resuming her original pace, Matty was left confused and concerned. He had thought she was cross at him and was relieved to find it was not so. Whatever the issue, it would have to wait as she clearly had no desire to take up the matter with him this day, and he had the rest of his plan to execute. So he turned back to face the church, and waited for the great brass bell to ring and the doors to open.

After a time, the sun having risen nearly to its zenith, the doors did open, though the bell had yet to sound.

Matty saw it was a group of about a dozen gents who slipped out quietly and trotted to the pine trees by the side of the church. There, they pulled out a number of sacks that had been stashed behind some of the trees and began emptying their contents onto the ground. They appeared to be costumes and props.

Matty smiled as he knew that these were the pace-eggers, preparing to provide their entertainment out on the street once it became filled with the villagers leaving the church. He recognized most of them, in fact it was the tavern keeper Richardson himself who was donning the guise of the Old Tosspot. This, of course, was the role Quentin was to have played before Lord Barnard hired him away for the present hunting trip.

Watching the players attempt to get themselves in order, a motley lot indeed, he could not help but think of his friend. He wondered what was transpiring out in the forest; what might have been discussed, decided, or done. He would have to speak with Quentin immediately upon their return, for no other person except Alexandra did he trust so well.

Quentin would give me a true account, he thought. *He also would have been a valuable source of counsel in my current undertaking.*

Kicking his toe into the soft verdant ground, Matty thought again about living in the woods where the men now hunted.

Would Alexandra ever go with me there, to live a life even less comfortable than the one she now endures? Could she bear a life with me at all? Either before today, or after?

His thoughts were broken by the pace-eggers, who took positions just behind him and to the left. He didn't want to be lost in the crowd that would assemble around them, so he moved farther off to the right. Just then, the church bell rang and the doors opened. Lady Barnard and Darnell, being in the front row, were among the last to leave, and in spite of Matty's attempts to be slightly apart from his fellow citizens, he was well-ensconced by the crowd by the time he spied the mismatched pair.

Matty began to navigate through the crowd to get near to them, yet Darnell saw his approach and tried to direct Lady Barnard away. She protested, however, as Lord Barnard had always insisted on a hasty exit in the past. Buoyed by the reception she enjoyed as she walked towards the church, she was in no hurry to get back to the gaol in which she lived. Further, she intended to meet up with Matty and looked for him, not knowing he had her in his sights already.

Darnell was left with no option save to attempt to intercept Matty, but he was no match for Matty's determined stride into Lady Barnard's company. He bowed again to her, finally addressing her directly.

"Lady Barnard, may I say what a privilege it is to see you in this brilliant sunshine. I've never seen a bonnet to match yours, nor a lovelier face for it to adorn."

Lady Barnard smiled and blushed, then forcibly removed her pleasure from her face. "You are called Matthew, is that so?" she asked with an air of nobility she had rarely displayed before, and could barely pass off as genuine.

"By my friends I am known as Matty, and I am your grateful servant, my lady," Matty replied.

Darnell began to interject, but was cut off by the pace-eggers, who announced that their production was about to start. Lady Barnard inquired to Matty what was to come, but Darnell quickly answered instead.

"It is a coarse and farcical presentation, Lady Barnard," said Darnell, "quite beneath the standards of someone of your taste and stature. Perhaps now would be an appropriate time to return to the house." Darnell not only wanted to keep Lady Barnard from Matty, he also was concerned about Lord Barnard returning early to find the house vacant. He had tempted chance sufficiently just to bring her to church, and the reward having been worth the risk thus far, he was eager to mitigate the very real chance that his luck – and his livelihood – may soon run out.

"No, I should like to see it," said Lady Barnard. "Matty, will you stand with us to watch this play?"

"I should be delighted," he answered, and took his place on her right side. "Hear now, they will start with a tune, introducing each character in kind. Watch this rascal here with the needled tail. He'll give you more than a scratch if you've not some coins or eggs to give him."

Lady Barnard laughed and stared with eyes agape as the players took their places and fiddle, whistle, and drum combined with voices into song:

Here's one, two, three jolly lads all in one mind
We have come a-pace egging and we hope you'll prove kind
We hope you'll prove kind with your eggs and strong beer
For we'll come no more nigh you until the next year

And the first that comes in is Lord Nelson you'll see
With a bunch of blue ribbons tied round by his knee
And a star on his breast that like silver do shine
And I hope he remembers it's pace egging time

And the next that comes in, it is Lord Collingwood
He fought with Lord Nelson till he shed his blood
And he's come from the sea old England to view
And he's come a-pace egging with all of his crew

The next that comes in is our Jolly Jack Tar
He sailed with Lord Nelson all through the last war
He's arrived from the sea, old England to view
And he's come a-pace egging with our jovial crew

The next that comes in is old miser Brownbags
For fear of her money she wears her old rags
She's gold and she's silver all laid up in store
And she's come a-pace egging in hopes to get more

And the last to come in is Old Tosspot, you see
He's a valiant old man and in every degree
He's a valiant old man and he wears a pigtail
And all his delight is a-drinking mulled ale

Come both ladies gay and dear sirs so refined
Put your hands in your pockets if you're of the mind
Put your hands in your pockets and treat us all right
If you give naught, we'll take naught, farewell and
good night

If you can drink one glass, then we can drink two
Here's a health to Victoria, the same unto you
Mind what you're doing and see that all's right
If you give naught, we'll take naught, farewell and
good night

Lady Barnard delighted in each successive character more than the one who'd come before. To Darnell's consternation, she and Matty laughed together, pointing at the players' fantastic antics. When Old Tosspot came around with a pail for favors, Lady Barnard – well warned about his sharp tail yet happy to pay for such spirited entertainment – scampered about herself, looking for something to give. Though she was the wealthiest person in attendance this day, without her husband beside her it was not appropriate for her to carry money.

Darnell, with neither a will to give nor anything to offer, had backed up a few steps to avoid being struck should Old Tosspot wield his weapon. Matty, better prepared and intent on impressing, had kept a couple of pence in his pocket, which he casually and accurately pitched into the pail. Refusing to be excused, Lady Barnard settled on the only thing of value besides her jewelry with which she could part: her bonnet. She held it out to Old Tosspot, who accepted it with a deep bow and delighted the crowd by donning it himself.

Within a few minutes, the entire crowd had been solicited, the eggs and coins collected, and all had escaped being pricked. The townspeople began to scatter, as holiday lunches were ready to be served. Darnell stepped forward to take Lady Barnard's arm, yet was rebuffed.

"Thank you, no, Darnell," said Lady Barnard. "I wish to discuss some matters with Matty." She laughed at her unintentional play on words, and enjoyed saying his name. "I shall see you later back at the house."

Darnell began to protest, but realized he had no argument. "As you desire, Lady Barnard," he said quietly.

Lady Barnard addressed Matty next. "The noonday sun is hot, Matty, and without my bonnet my head feels afire. May we sit under those trees?" She pointed to the pines where the pace-eggers, now on their way to the next village, had earlier assembled their costumes and props.

"Let me lead the way, Lady Barnard," said Matty. As they walked together towards the trees, neither noticed that Darnell, having started down the road towards the Barnards' home, had turned back and walked around the rear of the church, emerging near the spot where Matty and Lady Barnard sat. Matty removed his jacket and laid it on the ground so that Lady Barnard could sit without soiling her dress. Staying out of sight, Darnell tried to listen to their conversation.

"I have noticed you in the yard, Matty. Yet I don't know why I haven't met you until now."

"Where I work is not a place for such a fair one as yourself," Matty responded. "The horses are lovely, yet their smell is offensive. Quite unlike you, my lady, whose perfume is as delightful as her face."

Another smile, another blush, but an air of vulnerability now served to color her words. "Matty, I have been inspired by the season to begin my life anew. I want to dissolve the habits and routines that have kept me from truly experiencing the joys of living. There are things I've only begun to feel and I want to know them fully realized, rather than as fantasies in my imagination. Do you understand my meaning?"

"If the honor of sitting alone with you is part of this process of renewal, then I wholeheartedly support your efforts," said Matty. "I have often seen you in the window looking out" – at this Lady Barnard looked down, ashamed and embarrassed – "but never could I have imagined your true beauty until I met you today face to face."

"I dare say I have never been so bold, Matty, but my desire is great and my time is short. As you know, I could order you to do what I command, but I prefer to ask you as a favor. Matty, I should like to be alone with you this evening. In my home, in my quarters. In my bed. I know very little about what goes on in this town, but I know you are well versed in the practice of…of…intimate relations." A pause and a swallow. "I want you to do that with me."

To Matty, this was almost beyond comprehension. Lady Barnard was doing his scheming for him. He had planned to use all his powers of romantic persuasion to try to bed Lady Barnard, and here she was all but throwing herself at him with lustful abandon. It was almost as if someone were laying a trap for him, yet his intention was to be snared anyway, so what could it matter should it be true?

Still, it was important to ensure her consent, so he decided to parry with some of the mild protestations he so often had successfully fended off himself.

"Lady Barnard, your request is so grand it should be sufficient to satisfy all my dreams and desires. But surely, you are Lord Barnard's wife, as the ring on your finger –", and with that Matty saw that Lady Barnard's ring finger was barren. "Well," Matty continued, "as you are Lord Barnard's wife surely it wouldn't do for a stable hand to be seen accompanying you into your house."

"Matty, just as well you know I am Lord Barnard's wife, you know that Lord Barnard is not at home. Nor is he expected for another day. Furthermore, it is common knowledge that Lord Barnard favors you and has had you in our home many times. So you will know where to find me. The only remaining concern is when. Surely evening would be better, yet not too late for I will need time to make sure all is right in the house before morning. When you count three stars in the sky, come to the rear door. It will be unlocked and no other servants will be about. Are we agreed?"

Matty smiled, took her hand, and gently kissed it. Then he rose and helped her to her feet. He picked up his jacket and brushed the dirt and grass from the cloth. "My lady, I will do everything in my power to make this night one you will long remember. May I now escort you home?"

Lady Barnard made a small curtsy and held up her hand, awaiting his arm. Together they began walking towards the Barnard residence. When they had traveled out of view, Darnell emerged from his hiding place in the wood. He had not heard everything – was not close enough and his head still hurt from the night before – yet he had heard sufficiently to be shocked and appalled. His long resentment of Matty, so briefly transformed into a bemused tolerance, was instantly inflamed into a searing hatred. His ire caused him to tremble and he threw himself to the ground in a bitter stew of anger, hurt, and a searing desire for revenge.

After a few moments, his emotions had peaked and he was soon capable again of rational thought. He knew what he must do, and it not only was his duty as Lord Barnard's trusted servant, but also the ultimate strategic assault in his long, losing war with Matty, the thing that would be most likely to earn him the spoils he sought: a higher position among the Barnards, a greater reputation among the citizenry, and most important of all, Alexandra and her baby. Yes, he knew what he must do.

I must find Lord Barnard and tell him about this horrific conspiracy. That surely will prove the end of Matty's tenure in the village. But what about Lady Barnard? She will be hurt as well. Yet she, too, has betrayed me, used me to get to that...that detestable rogue. She, too, is guilty. She, too, must suffer.

However, Darnell was not a rider – even if he were, to get a horse he would have to get one from Matty, which would be impossible (and a complication Lord Barnard could not have foreseen when he instructed Darnell to ride to him). Therefore, to get to the hunting party in time for them to ride back into town and catch the would-be lovers in the act, he would have to run, walk, and swim as fast as possible.

This, then, is my test, he thought. *But first I must change into more comfortable clothing and eat something to give me energy.*

Darnell then rose and headed quickly back to his room in the cellar of the Barnards' house. Once there, he opened a small icebox and took out half a loaf of bread and a block of cheese and placed them on his table. He filled a skin with water, then removed his Easter clothing. Donned whilst in a pained panic, his wardrobe had seemed like royal robes as he and Lady Barnard traveled to church.

Now, they lay hastily strewn in a pile on the floor, ill-suited to the athletic task that awaited him.

Darnell dressed in lighter pants and a woven wheat-colored shirt. He replaced his finest shoes with worn leather boots cut low below his calves. He stuffed a handkerchief in his pocket and quickly tore off pieces of bread and chunks of cheese. He ate noisily and with as little contentment in the flavor as he felt about the recent events.

While he chewed, Darnell rehearsed what he would say to Lord Barnard, knew he would have to speak quickly and clearly, and with such urgency that his master would not think to question him about whether Lady Barnard had been to church. If he did, Darnell knew he would have to construct a story that absolved him of all blame.

Not that he was unwilling to accept any consequences for his role in breaking Lord Barnard's rule, but it was more important that Matty be disciplined. He assumed that Lord Barnard would ultimately feel obligated to reward him for revealing this plot. And even if not, even if Darnell's loyalty only tempered the severe decree his master would issue him for taking Lady Barnard to church against his orders, with Matty gone at last Darnell knew he could more easily endure Lord Barnard's wrath.

The bread and cheese consumed, Darnell swallowed the contents of his skin, then refilled it and placed it over his head and onto his shoulder for the journey. Taking Quentin's hand-sketched map, he wiped his mouth, shook crumbs off his clothing, and drew a deep breath, visualizing the challenging journey that awaited him. Finally, the loyal house servant left his dark quarters and set off at the sun's height for the deep woods.

Chapter 14

After Lord Barnard shot the hare, Quentin killed two more and the men walked back to the camp in silence. As before, each indulged the comfort and company of his own individual thoughts.

Quentin was consumed with concern for Matty and wished he could leave the hunting party and ride back into town to warn his friend about what had transpired. He would gladly conspire with him on a plan of escape. Quentin knew the forests bordering the town, and some well beyond, better than anyone he knew. He could help to provision and protect the man who once had saved his life. If only there was a way to reach Matty before Lord Barnard returned. Yet that would call for potentially drastic measures he wasn't comfortable undertaking, at least not until he had had a chance to speak with Matty himself.

As for Lord Barnard, he was wading within two streams of thoughts: one, of course, involving Matty and how he would begin his tutelage and thereby transform the stable hand into a gentleman as respectable in his comportment as he was fair in his features. The other stream involved his wife. If his orders were being heeded, she would be in the house while the townspeople, having survived Reverend Collins' judgmental harangues, would take in their inane entertainment in the village square. He fully intended to hold Darnell responsible should she venture outside, though surely there should be a severe punishment for her as well, if indeed she dared to flout his authority.

Lord Barnard had long assumed that he would grow to love his wife, and that they would have more successful and productive relations. Instead, he found her increasingly withdrawn, unresponsive, and bitter. Though he knew she was attractive, and was at heart a kind person, he did not enjoy being in her company; did not know, perhaps, how to engage with her socially. She knew nothing of his work and his interests, and he cared not about hers.

The plain fact, which he perhaps could not acknowledge or articulate, was that Lord Barnard simply preferred to be alone. Having largely been left by his childhood peers to amuse himself, he had never fully developed the attributes of empathy and patience that true friendships require. The one time he came closest to having such a relationship – with Peter Williams – fate callously took it away from him.

It was his wife's fault, he knew. Yet this was their life together and though it be unsatisfactory, it was something they, each in his or her own way, had to endure. Thus, Lady Barnard remained his wife largely because a nobleman requires a wife and she at least was compliant, generally being as invisible as he wished her to be. Yet lately she had seemed even less content, more complaining than was her wont, which is why he was concerned, for the first time really, that she would defy his order and go to church. Was this prescience or paranoia, of which Finster had once accused him when his client spoke of his distrust of the citizenry and their presumed gossip about him?

Well, he reasoned to himself as they reached the camp, *it is Easter morning and I should know some short time after we have consumed breakfast whether or not my orders have been obeyed – assuming, of course, that Darnell comes without delay as I had instructed.*

Quentin stoked the fire and prepared the hares. Using his sharpest knife, he removed the heads and feet, then made a slit in the belly and carefully cut around the midsection. With a tug, he removed half the animal's pelt over its hind legs, finally cutting off the tail to separate the fur from the rear. Then he turned the carcass around and did the same with the front half of the pelt. (Only Lord Barnard observed Quentin's skilled work, the others being put off by the blood.)

Reclaiming his knife, Quentin gutted the hares, pulling out the innards. Before bringing the stripped, disemboweled animals to the stream to wash them, he dug a hole about fifty paces away from the camp in which to bury the heads, feet, skin, and organs. Then he washed the carcasses in the stream, peeling off bits of silver skin and tossing them into the water.

Back at the fire, Quentin placed a grid of live, wet branches over the fire and placed the hares on top. They took long enough to cook for the men to regain their appetite and enjoy the fresh, tasty meat. After the meal was finished, the bones were placed in the hole Quentin had dug and the men went to bathe in the stream. With no sight nor sound of Darnell noted by any of the party, Lord Barnard finally had reason to believe that all was well. In fact, Darnell's absence so pleased him – for numerous reasons – that he vowed to make the most of their last full day in the forest. He suggested that they venture deeper into the woods in search of larger game, and asked Quentin to lead the way.

Quentin was uneasy about going farther away from town when what he most wanted to do was to get back at once. Yet he had no choice so, standing on the grassy hill where Lord Barnard and Finster had consummated their legal *coup d'corpse*, as it were, he raised a spyglass to the green depths that lay before them. Quentin knew in one direction they could reach a clearing only about half as far from their camp as their camp was to the town. From there they would have good visibility. He could lead them there by a circuitous route, making it seem farther than it actually was in the event he was able to escape. He would take the more direct route back and be able to place distance between himself and the others so as to reach Matty first.

Quentin got supplies and ammunition together, and organized the men for the trek.

For her part, Lady Barnard returned home breathless and burning with anticipation. She did not believe she could wait until Matty arrived. She could not, in fact, believe the day had gone so harmonious with her desires. Never had she conceived such a complete plan of action and executed it so well. She boldly and confidently walked the streets of the town, gathered a crowd and kept them with her beauty and charm, and succeeded in attracting the attention of the handsome stable hand. From one perspective, the hardest part of her strategy had already been completed.

And yet, the consummation of her plan would, she knew, in fact be the most difficult. For she, who had long

experienced lovemaking to be a monotonous duty, would
be paired with one expert in the full palette of sexual hues
that only a true artist would know how to apply. She feared
her inexperience and lack of sophistication would show,
that she would not know how to please a man who had
been with so many knowing and vivacious maidens.

*Though I arranged this tryst through the influence
of my power over Matty,* she acknowledged, *I know that
once in bed, I will be the servant and he the master.*

In any event, her concerns and fears only
heightened her excitement and impatience, for this evening
she would feel the pleasures of the flesh as never before.
She would experience a reawakening of herself as a
woman, as a person capable and deserving of giving and
receiving carnal joy.

*I will at last know what other women experience,
what all – most – men desire, what has been kept from me
for all these years.*

From the heat of the day and that which she felt
from within, she was fairly drenched and so she drew her
own bath – how she loved being alone at last! It was hard
work heating well water in the laundry cauldron and
bringing bucketfuls up the stairs to fill her footed porcelain
tub, yet when she finally disrobed and penetrated the clear,

steaming water, the reward was more than sufficient to justify the effort.

Lady Barnard did not bring a cake of soap or a brush. She simply reclined in the tub, let her head fall back, half her hair falling in the water and half draping over the side, and let herself be consumed by liquid. She felt light – even her breasts floated! – clean, and pure. She imagined herself a fish, gently propelling herself along with graceful and fluid movements. She was smooth, colorful, curious. No longer was she Lady Barnard; rather, she was who she was before she married Lord Barnard. She was, simply, Mary. Her eyes were closed. Her body was wet. Her heart was full. She remained in the tub until she became cold. Then she rose, dried her body, applied perfume and powder, donned a robe, and waited for the sun to set. Waited for Matty.

Unlike Lady Barnard – unlike even himself – Matty was anxious. Sitting on a bench in the stable, he felt an odd uncertainty. It all had gone so well thus far. *Could my luck continue?* he wondered. The only task still awaiting him was one he was exceptionally adept at, one he enjoyed and experienced more than most. Yet it always was an activity he had initiated with someone who had captured his fancy. Lady Barnard was certainly an attractive woman for her age, had all the finest clothes, jewelry, and perfumes to enhance her appeal. But she was no rugged beauty like Alexandra, nor had she a face or a figure the likes of which he had been drawn to and had frequently pursued in this and other villages.

Still, pleasure is not the goal of this love act to come, Matty assured himself. *All that was important was that the act should occur. And that Lord Barnard should learn of it.*

Oh yes, Matty was well aware that Darnell was within earshot of his conversation with Lady Barnard after the pace-eggers had left the square. He knew that Darnell would be loyal to Lord Barnard if for no other reason than it would serve to eliminate the stone in his boot that Matty so enjoyed being. He could envision Darnell meeting Lord Barnard at the door as he always would, then requesting a private audience with which to address an urgent issue. Matty would wait in the stable with a saddlebag packed for Lord Barnard to come out and banish him. He would leave word for Quentin to meet him in the woods and help him get settled. He would stay there a month or so until the talk ebbed. Then he would send for Alexandra. And then?

Another town, another life, another new beginning. Just as before and, who knows, as it may one day be again.

He did not want to leave the village, but could not bear to stay as Lord Barnard's son. He did not even want to hurt Lord Barnard, but he knew he could not reason with him nor argue his desire away.

I have no position from which to fight, and no will merely to run away and risk capture, Matty acknowledged. *I will not resort to violence, but neither will I be cowardly or complacent.*

What he could do – would do – is to be the rogue his reputation had insisted he be. In that way, Lord Barnard would be confronted with and forced to admit the folly of his scheme. To save face, he would have no other choice but to send Matty away.

Perhaps it would even prove beneficial for all involved. Matty might inspire Lady Barnard to improve the quality and frequency of her lovemaking with her husband. Perhaps they would be able to conceive their own child, which surely would be preferable to adopting a full-grown man and posing as if he were their true offspring. Darnell would be better off without Matty, maybe even Alexandra would, too, if she chose not to join him in exile.

Maybe the change, the chance to be alone, would be good for me as well, he thought. *Maybe a new beginning was needed by all, and by fate it was left to me to orchestrate the renewal, to set these transformations in motion.*

Contemplating that this all was necessary and that he had no choice but to serve fate's decree, Matty began to feel less anxious. He had a job to do for which he was uniquely well-suited. And believing that this would be his final conquest in the town, he decided it should be enjoyed to the fullest. He thought again about Lady Barnard, that perhaps there was something appealing about the vulnerability she barely could conceal behind the façade of her presumed power, something irresistible about this particular trophy, to bed the wealthiest woman around, his employer no less, while her husband hunts game less than half a day's ride away. And as he saw her fair features in his mind, his pulse quickened, and he began to wish away the moments that stood between his growing desire and its eventual fulfillment.

No place in his mind just then was Alexandra, and her mysterious ailment. Yet she was in mind of him. Having left church early in haste, she went directly to the pond where Matty liked to bathe. Sitting on the edge of the water, she watched as gulls and hawks flew low over the flat, glistening surface looking for the perch and lake trout that called this serene body of fresh water home.

The pond was not a place Alexandra came to often, other than to fetch water for the wash when the Barnards' pump was in need of repair. Matty tried a number of times to entice her into the water with him, yet she always refused. As a girl, she had seen a playmate drown in such a pond. She remembered seeing her face when she was taken from the water. It was blue, the mouth agape, her expression frozen in a state of surprise. *At what,* Alexandra wondered for days. Since then, she had never gone into a body of water deeper than her finely formed calves.

Staring at the pond, she thought of her baby, who, like her childhood friend, was completely immersed in water. The thought of it frightened Alexandra, more than the pond itself threatened her own sense of well-being. The prospect of having a baby had concerned but not pained her. Now, the very idea, the sickening image, of a dead baby inside of her brought forth a wave of nausea. She closed her eyes and drew a deep, slow breath. The feeling departed, though she kept her eyes shut, desperately seeking to regain control of her senses.

Now she tried to imagine her baby again; not dead, asphyxiated by fluid inside her body, but rather alive and outside of her. She had done this before, of course, but now, for the first time, she continued to feel a dread. Would this child's father claim patrimony? Would another man love the child as his own? Would she be able to bear the stares and the gossip of the ladies of the town? Would the child grow to feel wanted and accepted, both in its home and in its community?

Alexandra began to despair. She opened her eyes and looked again at the pond. It was still. Not a ripple, nor a bubble. No fish kissed the surface, no birds pecked the barrier where the air gave way to water. She looked around her. Rocks, sticks, greenery. She had heard of an herb that a woman could chew if she wanted to end her pregnancy. There were a variety of plants growing at the shore near her. She grabbed a few, tore them desperately from their stems, and stuffed them into her mouth. She chewed quickly, but they were bitter and she gagged. Most of what she had tried to eat came out.

Now came the tears. They were the first she had shed. And the last she would allow. She was not, after all, a helpless victim. Would never permit herself to be one, nor to feel as one.

I carry inside of my body a life, and if that is a large responsibility – and surely it is that – then I will have to be as large, if not more so, she commanded herself.

If for whatever reason she never saw Matty again, his presence would still be palpable within her child. She would draw strength from such reminders of him, even as she lent her own to her baby.

There is a reason this has happened, she was convinced. *I must be equal to the challenges that await. I owe it to myself. To my baby. To Matty.*

She rose and walked back to her cousin's house to rest. The holiday would soon be over, and tomorrow there would be fresh washing to do.

Chapter 15

Darnell was lean in body, but no athlete. The midday sun and the weight of his skin of water bore heavily on him as first he ran, then, breathless and perspiring, slowed his pace to an urgent walk. Twice before he reached the edge of the woods he stopped to drink. After the second time, upon resuming his pursuit of the party he developed a cramp in his side. The pain was sharp, as if a colt unwilling to be shod struck him with its hoof. Again he stopped, wiping his face with his handkerchief. Soon he would be covered by the forest's canopy; the cool, moist, mossy air would comfort him. That thought, and the importance of his mission, drew him forward once more.

His mission, in effect and in truth, was to bring down his enemy. Darnell knew he could never defeat Matty in terms of physical force, or of beauty or personality. Instead, he would leverage his own strengths, among them responsibility, propriety, loyalty.

Surely Alexandra can understand that these qualities are the more important, he assured himself, *particularly now, in her present situation, needing as she does a reliable man who would be a faithful husband with stable employment.*

Darnell laughed to himself at his inadvertent pun on "stable."

At the very least, he thought, *the child wouldn't have to grow up with a father who smelled of horse dung. How fair Alexandra could desire someone who worked with horses is beyond my powers of comprehension.*

In truth, Darnell was rather afraid of the beasts, a trait he knew he shared with Lady Barnard. She, too, would be injured by his mission. But so be it. He'd indulged his fantasy of having her on his arm, and had done so at considerable risk. He owed her nothing and in reality there was no chance of her ever giving herself to him. Darnell's choice was clear, and his chance was now.

By eliminating Matty, I am almost assured of having Alexandra. He pressed on.

The forest terrain grew more uneven now. He tripped on thick cords of roots that lay tangled among the carpet of half-decomposed mahogany-colored leaves. Branches tugged at his clothing and scratched his cheeks. The sameness of the scenery – greens and browns, everywhere greens and browns – made him disoriented. Though Darnell had verbal directions and a hastily sketched map to guide him, he grew unsure of the way. He looked up to the sky to gauge the position of the sun, to find an afternoon star, yet it was a futile effort as he was ignorant of how to navigate by celestial points.

Darnell brought his gaze down again. Before him, a steep rise. The quill-and-ink lines on the map held no topographic information. Had they taken this hill? Could horses climb such a grade? Was it even so steep as it appeared, or was his weariness and uncertainty generating unfounded doubts?

At his feet, a long stick. Darnell bent down for it, bringing it vertical in front of him. The tip reached his collarbone. He would use the stick to provide balance and leverage as he climbed the hill. It seemed to work. Darnell was surprised to find the going none too strenuous. At the highest point he was able to see his position with greater clarity and perspective. In fact, the ground did not slope down much at all on the other side. Where he had been before was not the true level earth, but rather a low-lying valley. From his new vantage point, Darnell had a better view of the landscape and a surer sense of his footing.

He moved ahead.

By the angle of the sun's rays through openings in the forest canopy, even Darnell could tell that the day was waning into late afternoon. Before long, it would be dark. He would need to find the camp quickly. He stopped for another drink from his skin of water. Two gulps were all that remained. Still parched from his previous evening's alcohol consumption, it was insufficient to quench his thirst and quell the throbbing in his head. He sat down on a fallen oak to rest and think. Surely, the camp must be nearby. Darnell's head and legs ached. His back and feet were sore as well, and his clothes, soaked now with perspiration, hung heavily on his weary body.

If the camp is not near, he thought, *I am more likely to die on this very spot than ever to complete my task.*

At the nadir of his deepening despair, Darnell heard in the stillness that surrounded him the sound of water slapping gently against rocks. The stream! He reached for the map and saw the parallel horizontal squiggles that Quentin had drawn to represent the crossing. Close above it was an "X". The camp! A surge of adrenaline seemed to expand his veins and animate his limbs. Quickly he rose to his feet, and he followed his ears to the source of the luscious liquid sound. Running again, he soon saw the water, and it may as well have been the River of Jordan come to take him to freedom for the prayers of gratitude it elicited in the servant.

Finally he stood before it, almost disbelieving that he had actually reached this critical landmark on his arduous journey. Gurgling continuously with neither pause nor impatience, the stream was blissfully, peacefully oblivious to the frantic, desperately relieved form on its bank. Darnell dropped to his knees and all but thrust his head into the cool water. He cupped his hands and drank the most delightful brew he had ever been served.

Wiping his eyes and forehead, Darnell looked ahead and saw the small hill that he knew must be the site of the camp. Though he wished to remain and refresh himself longer, the target being so close he dared not delay a moment longer. He took one last drink, filled his skin with water, and then began to ford the stream, which was approximately ten horse lengths wide.

Midway across, it became deep enough to warrant a few swimming strokes. The current carried him somewhat, but he was able to maintain his direction. As he neared the other side, his sore feet – soaked and glad to be so – returned to the bottom and took him in labored strides towards and up the far bank. Again, Darnell silently expressed gratitude for the water that served him as both curative and compass.

As Darnell climbed the hill, leaves and dirt and twigs clung to his boots and legs as though he were a tree oozing sap. His profoundly improved spirits helped propel him quickly to the top where, sure enough, there was visible evidence of the camp: the rock-lined fire pit, the canvas tenting and blankets, personal effects in small, scattered piles. Yet there was no sign of Lord Barnard or the others in his party.

Perhaps they are still out hunting, he thought. He cocked his head to listen for gunfire but heard none. There was no way for him to tell how far and in which direction they had gone.

His mission was still incomplete, yet Darnell felt he had accomplished much simply by finding the camp before dark. The sun was less than a hand's breadth above the horizon.

The best thing to do is to stay here at the camp and await their return, he reasoned. In any event, he was too exhausted to search further. He laid his water skin on the ground and sat on a rock. It was hard and unfriendly.

Darnell turned to see the blankets sprawled on the ground around the fire pit. They looked far more inviting. Despite being soaking wet, he went and sat on one. He removed his boots, took off his shirt. He leaned back, supporting himself on one elbow. Soon he was lying flat.

The forest looked calm and beautiful. Darnell was pleased to have endured such an arduous adventure. He had met the demands of his test! He closed his eyes. He listened again for sounds from the party, but heard only the stream. He imagined himself lying on a raft in the middle of the stream. Birds singing, the water lapping, his breathing soft and slow. He had never felt so relaxed. He had never felt so safe. The raft floated gently downstream. Cradled by the earth, calmed by the violet sky, Darnell was at peace. And in seconds, he was asleep.

No gunshot ever awoke Darnell, for the party found nothing worth spending the powder. There were rabbits, woodchucks, and squirrels a-plenty, to be sure, but Lord Barnard's hunger was for larger prey. He wanted a trophy, a light meal wouldn't do. Yet nothing suitable was seen. No deer, no elk, no moose. The men rode on in hopes of finding game. Quentin was forced to go deeper into the woods than he had intended. And though it was essentially his responsibility to facilitate a successful hunt, Quentin was anxious to suggest that they cut short the day and head back to town.

Lord Barnard, however, was keen to continue. So much else had thus far gone so well that he insisted on pressing his luck. Surely a beast of some sort would spring into view. He would raise his firearm and with sure aim press the trigger. Two explosions – from the powder in his gun and from the tearing of the creature's flesh – would signify success. A third explosion, in his heart, would throw throbbing streams of blood throughout his body at the sight of the kill.

This strange man, stranger yet when he was younger, when he was too refined and aloof for the rough play of the boys at his school, those boys who teased him, those boys he had neither the strength of body nor the resolve to fight, this strange man now, with a gun in his hands, felt strong, virile, unconquerable. It was a rare feeling, and he would not release it willingly.

It was not blood that Lord Barnard was after. He loved the hunt because it produced trophies, physical proof of his manliness. The gun was his great equalizer. His wealth gave him leverage in his business relationships, but he was easily intimidated in social engagements. The unhealed scars of his youth he not only felt inside but also thought were obvious to others, as though they were a physical mark on his forehead – easy to spot and easy to disdain. But here, out in the woods, he could prove himself superior to his prey. With his intelligence, his sure trigger finger – and, of course, Quentin's eyes and instincts – he could compete, man against animal, and most times would emerge the victor.

No, to Lord Barnard a measly hare was insufficient spoils for his first hunting trip of the spring. It would never do. They must press on.

"Quentin," said he, "I have charged you with finding for us some game to hunt. Can it be there is no animal left in these woods that weighs more than my boots?"

"Surely it's quite odd, Lord Barnard," said Quentin. "Yet we have had enough for both dinner and breakfast. You supplied the latter yourself. May I suggest we call the hunt complete and head back to camp early?"

"I'll not hear of it," said Lord Barnard, "until I have shot something that stares at me with eyes as large as my own. I came to this spot to conduct some business in private and to hunt with my friends. The business has been concluded. The hunt has yet to be."

So Quentin led the party deeper into the forest, though he knew that it was getting too late in the day to find good game. He decided it would do no good to quarrel with Lord Barnard, who surely was experienced enough a hunter to come to this realization himself, once he surrendered his stubborn position. He finally did so as dusk descended, though he was unhappy about it and remained silent as they began to return to the camp.

Shrouded in a darkening veil, the day was too old, Quentin thought, to return to the village. They would have to bed down at the camp one more night and return in the morning light. Yet as they approached the high ground, the unexpected sight of Darnell's sleeping figure signaled that all was about to change.

Chapter 16

Matty changed. He washed himself, dressed in fresh, clean clothes. Additionally, he embraced his new attitude about the evening that awaited him. Or rather, he reclaimed anew his traditional attitude about romantic trysts. He felt bold, desirous, adventurous. He erased any lines drawn in his conscience around good and bad, right and wrong. He had composed a script that thus far had played out perfectly, and now he was ready to accept his cue to come on stage and fulfill the exciting final scene.

This is who I am, he told himself with no trace of modesty or shame. *This is what I do and I do it, as ever, for me and for my doomed brother as well.*

Leaving his room, Matty stepped behind the stable into the woods, just a few paces so as to pick some of the purple wildflowers that came up each spring. He carefully broke the stems, leaving white drops of succulence on the torn tips. Matty brought the flowers to his nose; satisfied with the scent, he walked towards the Barnards' house.

Lady Barnard, at her familiar place beside her window, sat in her silk robe and watched Matty's approach. She smiled, spying the flowers in his hand. Soon she would be the flower in his grasp. She prayed that her sight and scent would be as pleasing to him as the purple petals he now held. Her pulse accelerated, she felt the robe itself was pounding in time with her heart. Between her legs, a moist heat arose. He was nearly at the back porch, so she left the window and hurried down the stairs to meet him.

Halfway down, she stopped herself. She didn't want to be breathless and impatient. She was the Lady, he the servant. She must not betray her intense need, must at least feign the appearance of being in control. She took a deep breath, then saw the door handle turn. Lady Barnard elected to remain on the stairs, and struck a pose that was at once authoritative and inviting.

Matty, while crossing the yard to the Barnard house, had seen her sitting by the window. He had become accustomed to her looking at him, and had trained his upward peripheral vision to gaze back at her while appearing to look straight ahead. He could recognize a woman rabid with desire. Recalling Alexandra's testimony about the Barnards' bed sheets, he realized just how desperate she really must be for a man who could please her. It was just the sort of challenge on which he thrived.

It was, in fact, just the sort of situation on which he had made his reputation.

He took the final steps to the door with the same measured pace at which he had been walking. Without hesitation, he reached for the doorknob and turned it. The last time he did so it was on the orders of Lord Barnard. Now it was on the invitation of Lady Barnard. What had Lord Barnard ever offered in return for his service? Money, of course. Some favors, gifts, food, clothing. A nice room built just for him in the rear of the stable. Useful things, to be sure, but they paled in comparison to what Lady Barnard, standing on the staircase with her right hand on the rail and her left upon her hip, was about to tender.

He is beautiful, she thought, barely able to hide the short gasp of a breath she took as he closed the door behind him. *How shall it be,* she wondered? *Shall we sit and talk for a while? Are we to go immediately to my quarters? Would he carry me there? No, I mustn't wonder. I must be in control. I must initiate what is to be.*

"I am pleased you are punctual, Matty," she said, trying desperately to disguise her lust.

"The time since last we spoke has crawled as a snail, my Lady," Matty replied. "It was all I could do not to leap into the sky and draw the sun back down with me."

Matty walked over to the stairs. He stopped at the bottom, looking up at her. With the light from the chandelier candles casting an amber glow upon her, the thin, smooth material of Lady Barnard's robe outlined her figure. Matty could see that the robe was the sum total of all the clothing she wore. His blood, too, began to race. He wanted to leap up the steps to her and have her right then and there, but he knew he needed to demonstrate caution. This was a Lady in her house, and to ensure that any shred of what was to happen might possibly be defensible, he needed her to make the first move.

"Come here, Matty," said Lady Barnard.

Matty complied, more slowly and deliberately than either of them wanted. When they were standing on the same step, she turned, her right hand releasing the rail. Matty could wait no longer and took the slight change in her stance as an invitation. He took her in his arms and kissed her, powerfully, deeply, all the while their pounding hearts – now pressed together – kept time of each exquisite moment of their embrace.

When their lips parted, Lady Barnard's whole face – her mouth, her eyes, her brow – was moist with saliva, desire, and perspiration. Over her entire body, she felt her skin was alive, pulsing, afire. She was close to tears and her mind could not focus.

"I don't know what to say," she whispered, which was true; yet what she also was trying to express was that she did not know what to do. Matty understood and was more than ready to take control.

"Let us say nothing, nothing more," he said. "We must let our fleshes speak for us to each other."

With that, Matty, emboldened fully both in his mind and in his groin, lifted Lady Barnard into his arms and carried her up the steps, the purple wildflowers falling onto the space the two lovers to be had occupied. Lady Barnard was sure she should faint before they reached the top of the staircase. She hugged Matty around his neck and buried her head in his chest. She was his prize yet the reward would surely be hers.

Taking the final step, Matty turned and carried Lady Barnard past the sword rack directly to her room and placed her gently on her bed. A candle she had lit and placed on a small round table by her bedside flickered its greeting.

Lady Barnard had yet to release Matty's neck and drew him down to her that they might kiss again. This time, Matty's hands glided down the outline of her body that her robe had so teasingly revealed on the stairs. She felt his hands on her shoulders first, and tiny shocks such as one felt in winter when walking on the carpet shot off throughout her being as he felt the sides of her breasts. His hands continued to her waist sloping inward, then out again at her hips and down her thighs, which she parted slightly not only in invitation but also to welcome in cooler air to offset the blazing heat that seemed to be melting her from the inside.

Matty then broke the embrace, rose and saw the pleading and yearning in Lady Barnard's eyes. He began to remove his clothing and she watched him, her need banishing any embarrassment she might otherwise have felt. He soon stood naked before her, his blood-engorged penis jutting perpendicular from his body. In all their fumbling attempts to copulate, Lady Barnard had never seen with such clarity her husband's organ the way she now took in Matty's. Throbbing, bobbing, it seemed to have a life and will of its own. She wondered what it would do inside her. Unselfconsciously, instinctively, she spread her legs further apart.

Yet her robe was still a barrier between their bodies. Matty sat on the edge of the bed, reached over and untied the sash that kept the folds of her robe closed. Slowly, gently, he opened them, and Lady Barnard's pale nakedness glowed upon his face like a treasure revealed. Now it was his turn to gaze and Lady Barnard swore to herself that she could feel his eyes as fingers on her breasts and belly.

"I must have you," she said.

"And I you," he replied.

Matty lay beside her, on her left side, and burrowed his right arm beneath her neck. With his left hand, he traced the arc of her eyebrows, his fingertips barely brushing her skin. From there, they glided down the gentle curve of her nose, then pressed against her lips, which pursed and kissed his skilled, strong hands. With his first finger, he drew a circle around her chin, then tickled her throat, finally settling high on her chest, where the soft mounds of her breasts began. They heaved with her deep and rapid respirations, and he let them move against his open palm, occasionally bringing his fingers forward in a gentle squeeze.

He drew more circles, one on each areola. Her cinnamon nipples pointed like spires to heaven and he bent down to kiss and suck each one in turn. Lady Barnard could barely keep from shouting, such were the sensations pulsing from within her, her blood coursing like river rapids. She prayed he would reach her molten core soon, yet each slow second was agonizingly delicious.

Indeed, Matty quickened his pace and gave scant attention to her belly, nestling his fingers in the small hill of hair a hand's breadth below her navel. It was moist like morning dew, fragrant like marsh grass, and led to a warm, wet opening with thin petals splayed apart, welcoming him inside to seek its nectar. Matty's fingers explored her slick interior to their full length, taking stock of her feminine architecture, the sloping walls, deep passages, and sensitive spots in places never before sought and never before found.

Now Lady Barnard's eyes closed. Her right hand went to her mouth and she bit down hard on the meaty part of her thumb. Matty's glistening fingers led her left hand to his member, and she could feel the life surging through it. She traversed its length, gripped its girth, and marveled at the hard muscle he managed to keep hidden in his trousers.

Lady Barnard was on the edge of unconsciousness, Matty on the verge of climax. He rolled on top of her and guided his insistent sword into her sopping sheath. Lady Barnard was silent no more. Of just how she expressed herself she had no sense; it was moaned gibberish and guttural breaths that filled the room, yet all she heard was her own blood rushing through the tiny vessels in her ears.

Matty gave two gentle pokes, embedding himself halfway and withdrawing nearly fully each time; on the third thrust he plunged to the hilt. Lady Barnard's vagina took his length, smothered and embraced it, moistened it, and let it go, only to draw it back in again. Her heels rested in the pits behind his knees. She kicked him forward into her as a desperate rider drives his boot heels into a horse's ribs. Her arms squeezed his neck, pulled his hair. With his left elbow driven into the mattress to maintain his balance and position, Matty was able to reach his right hand around to pull and squeeze at her buttocks.

He, too, grunted and wheezed, yet there were more sounds emanating from the couple than those that flowed from their mouths. Her wetness was sufficient to make slurping, slapping noises with each stroke in and out. Their sweaty bellies clapped with each thrust and the bed itself seemed to squeal with delight. The primordial aroma of lovemaking wafted everywhere. Matty's pelvis pivoted more quickly, Lady Barnard's met each parry. They began pounding against each other faster and faster, then Lady Barnard thrust her buttocks off the mattress and emitted a shrill cry. Her vagina gripped Matty's penis as a milkmaid works a teat, and Matty shouted as his seed shot in rapid spurts deep into her canal.

"Let us say nothing, nothing more," Matty had advised on the staircase. To this they remained true as they concluded their coupling. Their eyes met, their lips came together in a final, gentle kiss, and as Matty slipped out of her and half off of her body, the two lovers breathed heavily in unison, the exhaustion from their exertions overtaking their passion. Matty drew the coverlet over their bodies and he tenderly stroked her belly.

For the first time in her life, Lady Barnard was fully satisfied yet she was still too consumed in the aftershocks of their lovemaking to speak or show her gratitude to Matty. No matter, for within minutes the two lovers were asleep. To this extraordinary performance, there would be no encore.

Chapter 17

The footsteps he heard clearly enough, but were they real or a part of his dream? On the cusp of consciousness, Darnell slowly opened his eyes. Despite the dark sky in the background, he quickly understood that it was the end of a rifle he was looking into. Directly behind the weapon's black shaft he could see Quentin's squinting face. Again unsure whether this was true or illusory, he wisely chose to remain still, testing the persistence of the image by closing his eyes and opening them again.

At the same time that Darnell concluded he was indeed trapped at gunpoint, Quentin recognized the strange figure asleep at their camp site as his client's house servant. "It is Darnell, Lord Barnard," Quentin reported.

"Darnell?" Lord Barnard responded, in a voice at once shocked, irked, and concerned. He pushed his way past his friends, whose craned necks peered over Quentin's shoulders even as they kept their bodies safely behind the armed guide. From Darnell's dazed perspective, this gave Quentin the appearance of being a many-headed beast. Finally, Lord Barnard and Darnell were face to face. This was the moment at which Darnell's courage and resolve were to be most strenuously tested. Fail this test, he knew, and no other would matter.

"Well? What is it? What brings you here, and why now?" Lord Barnard's words came quickly and with rhythmic emphasis. Darnell was ill-prepared to deliver the news under such intense inquisition, yet he knew he was not to lead this conversation. Still, he managed to raise himself onto his elbows to better give himself breath and a little more space with which to speak his testimony.

"I have traveled a long, hard journey on foot to tell you urgent news regarding Lady Barnard and Matty Musgrave," Darnell began in measured tone and meter. Looking at the mute gawking faces, he added in a softer voice, "Perhaps we should speak alone."

"Out with it!" Lord Barnard commanded.

Thus chastened, Darnell continued at a more rapid pace. "I am sorry to report to you, sir, that they have conspired with each other to undertake a tryst that likely is happening at this very moment. In your own house," he added for emphasis.

Lord Barnard's eyes grew to wide white circles that the growing darkness was helpless to obscure. He plunged his arms down to Darnell, grabbing his shoulders with both hands and raising his servant's upper body off its elbows.

His pursed lips held back a bilious screech even as a couple of drops of spittle eked through. Several silent moments ensued, with no man daring even so much as to exhale.

Finally, Lord Barnard released Darnell, who fell back flat, then quickly brought himself up to a sitting position and put on his still-damp shirt.

"Fetch a torch," Lord Barnard finally ordered. Two of the men scrambled in the darkness to find a thick branch, then flailed about trying to light it aflame. When they succeeded in getting it lit, they brought it back to where Lord Barnard and Darnell remained mute and unmoving.

"Tell me exactly what has occurred, Darnell," Lord Barnard demanded.

"I overheard Lady Barnard and Matty speaking this morning. He was flirting with her, and she with him. I heard them make plans to meet in your house this evening."

"Where did they speak to each other?" inquired Lord Barnard. "Did Lady Barnard leave the house against my orders?"

Now Darnell had to tread carefully, for to admit that she did would only incriminate himself. He knew he might not escape punishment, yet he did not want to dilute the blame that Lord Barnard must find with Matty primarily, and his wife secondarily.

"Yes, Lord Barnard, but under my careful guidance," he said. "She so wanted to see how people were dressed and therefore I escorted her to the front porch. Merely to watch until they had traveled beyond our view to church," Darnell was quick to add. "It was not my intention that she should speak with anyone, but Matty saw us and came over. I didn't believe that Matty meeting us on the porch would violate your orders, yet when they began to make their plans, I knew I must come to you at once. Had I a horse and could ride competently, I would have arrived here sooner. But if you hurry back to town, I am certain you will find them together in the most despicable of circumstances."

It was a good lie, plausible, and rendered quite believably by Darnell. The moments of silence during which Lord Barnard fought to maintain his composure had enabled Darnell to compose himself as well, yet he was unsure whether the lie was accepted, as Lord Barnard committed himself to no verbal response for several moments longer. Finally, he called his solicitor over.

"Finster. Bring my satchel." Finster did as he was told. Lord Barnard grabbed the bag from him and pulled out the papers the two had prepared the day before.

"You see this document, Darnell?" he asked his servant. Darnell nodded. Lord Barnard continued. "By this document, I have made Matthew Musgrave my legal heir. He is to be my own son, do you understand?" Again, Darnell nodded. Again, Lord Barnard resumed his declaration.

"If what you say here is true, I will cross out Matthew's name and write yours instead. Finster here will witness and notarize it, and my fortune will in time pass to you instead of to him. However, if what you say is a lie, I will kill you. With neither hesitation nor remorse. Do you understand that?"

Darnell swallowed hard, but spoke firmly. "Lord Barnard, I have ever been loyal to you. As much as it pains me to bring this news to you, you who already have been as a father to me, I swear to you that what I tell you is true, and that you will have proof waiting for you in your own home, if only you will hurry to it."

"Quentin, gather our horses and all our belongings," ordered Lord Barnard. "We are returning to town at once. Finster, get a pen and ink." With that, in front of Finster and Darnell, Lord Barnard did as he promised. He substituted Darnell's name for Matty's, and Finster signed the document again. "Hear this, Darnell," warned Lord

Barnard, "if you are wrong, you will hold this paper over your heart, and I will thrust my sword through its center until my blade exits through your back. If you are right – and I have known you long enough to believe that you must be – this paper guarantees that you are heir to my estate."

"You must hurry back if you are to view the evidence, Lord Barnard," said Darnell. "You will then see that I am speaking the truth."

"Indeed we shall," said Lord Barnard. "Quentin, are we ready?"

"Yes, Lord Barnard," Quentin replied. Stunned by Darnell's words, and fearful of what may come to pass, Quentin realized there was nothing he could do to save Matty from his fate. No matter how quickly or expertly he rode, he could not arrive back in town long enough before the others to help Matty make his escape. His only hope was to warn him in advance of their arrival, and the only way to do that was to use his horn when they emerged from the woods. But to do that would surely result in a severe response from Lord Barnard.

Quentin was torn, and not in the least because he knew his friend so well. Matty courted danger just as surely as he courted women, and he could neither be changed nor dissuaded from who he was and what he chose to do. Never had Quentin known a man whose destiny seemed so much of his own making, and while that made Matty all the more appealing – to Quentin as a friend, and to countless women as a lover – it also necessarily left impotent any intimate of Matty's who might hope to wield an influence on him.

"Darnell, you will ride with Quentin," Lord Barnard ordered. "Everyone else, mount your horses and stay close, for we shall wait for no one. True, it is dark and the woods are thick, but we must make haste."

Clumsily, Darnell tried to mount Quentin's horse but needed the concerned guide's assistance to get on securely. "Hold on tight, it will be rough going until we reach a clearing," advised Quentin.

Then at once, the entire party plus Darnell shot out towards the town, Quentin necessarily in the lead as he best knew the way, with Lord Barnard just half a length behind. No one spoke as they rode, yet all understood that something quite scandalous had occurred, involving Lord Barnard's wife. Improper a topic as it would be for public discussion or even with their own wives, it would be something to snicker about in private with customers, colleagues, and friends. Knowledge of this inflamed Lord Barnard's paranoia, while adding heat to his raging anger.

Finster, though he was well aware of Matty's reputation, still was shocked to think that he would have the pluck to ply his romantic trade with his employer's wife. Though he did feel some satisfaction in that he had held the correct opinion about Matty's suitability as an heir, he had not much higher a regard for Darnell. Had the circumstances been quite different than they were, Finster would have felt compelled to caution his client about the change made hastily on the legal document.

Darnell, his arms wrapped tightly around Quentin's torso, felt such an exhilaration that his loyalty was to be rewarded that he momentarily forgot his fear of riding on horseback. In fact, he had barely the clarity of mind to realize what Lord Barnard had meant about this document he was defiling with a quill, applying the brute force one might use to gut a deer.

Crossing out Matty's name and writing my own, what did he say? Legal heir? Own son? Me? This was to be my reward? And had I not acted, what then? I would have had to serve Matty? What insanity had come over Lord Barnard anyway?

Difficult though it was to make sense of the details, Darnell seized upon the end result: he would stand to inherit Lord Barnard's estate. He would be a servant no more. Surely Alexandra would have no choice, no other desire, than to devote her life to him.

My enemy gone, Darnell thought, *my love won, and a fortune as well. Victory is mine. At last, I have prevailed!*

Quentin, navigating through the darkened woods at quite a quicker pace than he would otherwise advise, gave no thought to – nor really felt – Darnell's arms clasping him tight around his belly. He thought only of Matty, tried to imagine the situation in which he would be found, and despaired of being able to help the man who once had saved his own life. Quentin resolved that whatever Matty's punishment (banishment he assumed; to bring charges of adultery would only further bring shame and scandal to Lady Barnard), he would bear it with him. Together they would go elsewhere, perhaps back to these woods that he knew so well.

My son, Lord Barnard lamented to himself, *how, my son, could you have abused my love for you? I have always treated you fairly, favorably even. I was prepared to give you all I own, yet you have taken the one thing most rightfully mine.*

He imagined Matty lying in bed with Lady Barnard. He could picture the scene, but had no frame of reference with which to assign a look of blissful fulfillment on her face. Yet he knew somehow that Matty could do – likely had done – what he himself had never been able to accomplish. And the hurt and disappointment he'd been feeling were swept away by a torrent of anger.

He tightened his grip on his reins. A flash of red appeared before his eyes – perhaps a surge of blood flowing through his veins. He replayed these thoughts in his mind repeatedly, unable to shake it free so as to enable a new idea to enter. Before long, however, the approaching border between the woods and the village sharpened his focus on the here and now, as opposed to what may already have occurred.

Suddenly, a keening wail was heard, jarring him from his perseveration. Lord Barnard cocked his head to identify the source of the sound. Again he heard it, though now he looked ahead and saw it was Quentin, his brass horn to his lips. *He is trying to warn Matty*, he realized. Each gallop bringing the party closer to his house, Lord Barnard would not allow a third blast from the horn.

He reached for his gun, which had held an unused shot for hours now. Darnell was hunched over, looking down, leaving Quentin's head in full view. Lord Barnard saw him draw another breath, then he pulled the trigger. Quentin's breath never reached the horn. Instead, his head swung back, his left arm, with which he held the horn while using the right to control the reins, flung overhead, the horn itself becoming a projectile that hit Upham square on the forehead. Though stunned for a moment, the tailor managed to maintain his mount. Now Quentin's upper body jerked forward, slumped over his horse's neck. Slowly he began to slide off the horse to the ground, lifeless as the cold dirt that awaited him.

The only thing momentarily keeping Quentin on his horse was Darnell, who had yet to loosen his grip. But when he raised his eyes to see streams of blood flowing down Quentin's back, he drew his arms back quickly (nearly unsteadying himself) and watched in horror as Quentin fell off. He could hear the horses behind him kicking and stepping on Quentin's body as they passed it, as if it were no more consequential an obstacle than a branch or stone.

Instinctively, Darnell grabbed the reins and secured himself on the horse. Frightened as he was to find himself in control of a galloping horse, he was more stunned still by Quentin's ghastly murder, evidence of which dripped down Darnell's face. (Had he not mistaken it for sweat, surely Darnell would have fainted and fallen to the ground to be trampled to death.)

Dear God, he thought, *if this is how Lord Barnard punishes Matty's friend, how much more savage a sentence must await Matty?*

Darnell had not considered that Lord Barnard's rage could turn lethal. He began to fear the confrontation to which they raced ever closer. True, Darnell wished to be rid of Matty yet it was not his death he desired; expulsion would have been more than sufficient. Yet it was clear to him that it was impossible to challenge Lord Barnard in his present emotional state.

Now at the head of the group, and with his house in sight, Lord Barnard gestured with his right arm for all the riders to slow down to a trot. Though Darnell lacked the skill to control Quentin's horse, the well-trained beast instinctively followed the pace of its peers. They stopped at the edge of the property to the rear of the house. Lord Barnard asked Finster and Darnell to follow him but to wait downstairs. He gave leave to the others to return to their homes. Slowly, silently, the three approached the house, Darnell clutching his empty water skin, Finster carrying his client's satchel, Lord Barnard gripping his gun.

Chapter 18

In the beginning, there was darkness. The end, presumably, is encased in darkness as well. But no matter how deep and absolute a darkness may be, it inevitably is overcome by light. Not all at once, but slowly, gradually. As one advances, the other recedes, and the one coming into power will in time be the one to surrender.

Such are the cycles of the days. Such are the cycles of life itself.

Picture a figure lying in blissful unconsciousness. To him, light and substance are not merely hidden, they are infinitely void, like a starless sky in the deep black of space. Yet from this vast emptiness, this enormous absence, slowly builds an awareness. A subtle change in tone and hue. The blackness gives way to warmer shades. Now it is brown, like a horse. Then red, like blood. Now orange, like the morning sun. Then yellow, like candlelight.

Candlelight is familiar. It has not only luminescence but a scent as well. Stirring two senses now, it acts upon the prone figure. Consciousness rises, sleep subsides. The eyes slowly open. There is the light. And there, in front of the light, is a figure. Because the light is behind the figure, no features are visible. A featureless figure can well prove to be a figment of one's imagination, and so the eyes close again, then reopen. The figure remains. The eyes open further. They focus more sharply. And within the dim nimbus, the figure soon becomes recognizable. It is Lord Barnard, standing at the foot of the bed and pointing a gun directly between those eyes.

Those eyes, of course, belong to Matty, lying still in Lady Barnard's bed. To his right, in his arms, is the naked figure of Lady Barnard herself. Warm, soft, sleeping, she is a study in bliss. In front of Matty stands a present danger. At his side, a sweet memory. Becoming clear-headed again, he understands the situation. He had schemed for such a confrontation, though he had expected it would happen later, on more neutral ground. When he was better prepared and less blatantly guilty.

So, the final scene is to be played here, now, in full view, thought Matty as he surveyed the scene. *I had hoped it would be enacted on the morrow, in daylight, standing, face to face, eye to eye, man to man. Yet it is as well that Lord Barnard need not rely on rumor or hearsay. The evidence of my offense is laid bare before him. The next move is his to make. Then it will be mine.*

"Tell me, Matthew," Lord Barnard said with mock generosity. "How do you find my feather bed? My pillows, my sheets? Are they comfortable? Are they well to your liking?"

Sitting up, Matty would concede no disadvantage in this remarkable situation in which he found himself. "I do like your feather bed, Lord Barnard," Matty replied confidently. "The pillows are soft and the sheets are warm. I've not known such comfort before."

"And tell me further, Matthew," said Lord Barnard, now raising his voice and speaking with clenched jaw, "how do you enjoy my lady, asleep beside you? How is it to lay with my wife?"

Matty spoke calmly and slowly. "Unlike the comfort of your bed, Lord Barnard, many fine women have I known. Yet your lady gay stands alone for the sheer depth of her desire and the tenderness of her caresses. I do envy you...master," he said half-tauntingly.

"Arise, you scoundrel," shouted Lord Barnard, waking his wife. "For this insult, this gross disrespect, you will die!"

At the sound of her husband's voice, Lady Barnard sat up quickly, her breasts falling on the covers that laid on her belly. Feeling the night air on her exposed flesh, she hastily drew a blanket up to her neck. She attempted to speak, but Matty bade her to hold her peace by placing his hand on her still-exposed bare shoulder.

"If you so desire to kill me, you need only to pull your trigger, Lord Barnard," said Matty, doubting Lord Barnard's resolve in light of the affection he had always shown his trusted stable hand.

"It shall never be known in fair England that Lord Barnard slew an unclothed man," replied Lord Barnard. "Now, get up and get dressed."

"And then what?" challenged Matty. "Will you do greater honor to yourself in shooting an unarmed man simply because he is not naked?"

Lord Barnard walked out the door of Lady Barnard's room and into the hallway, where his sword rack was stationed. He removed the top two – the finest two, which he himself had bought yet never planned to use – and returned to the room.

This action was observed silently by Darnell and Finster, who had dutifully been waiting downstairs. From there they had heard the confrontation coming from within Lady Barnard's room. Now, seeing Lord Barnard take weapons for an apparent duel, they felt compelled to risk his ire and ascend to the second floor to try to avert a second murder. (For his part, Finster was already

conceiving a defense of Lord Barnard for his shooting of
Quentin.) On their way up they stepped on the fallen purple
wildflowers that lay scattered on the stairs.

"It is true you have nary a pocket knife," Lord
Barnard said to Matty, "against such fine long beaten
swords as these. But you shall have the better of the two
and I the worse. Thus you have your chance not only to
survive but to succeed. But I say that my skill shall triumph
over your pluck, and this dishonor you have brought to me
and to my wife shall pass away even as your blood shall
leave your body with every last beat of your roguish heart."

At this point, Darnell and Finster reached the
doorway. Lord Barnard sensed their presence but rather
than turn away from his opponent, he merely waved the
sword he was to use to keep them in their place. With his
left hand, he held out the sharper, shinier sword to Matty,
who arose from Lady Barnard's bed and side, donned his
pants and shirt, and took the weapon reluctantly, for no
swordsman was he.

Has it come to this end, Matty thought anxiously.
*Has my plan worked too well, or not at all? I have never
dueled another man in my life, and now am I to die before
the eyes of the hated Darnell and the barrister chap?*

Where are the others in the party? he wondered. *Where is Quentin?*

"Here is how it shall be," said Lord Barnard. "You will have the first blow, and I'll defend it if I can. If so, I shall take the next blow, and a fatal one I intend it to be."

"You would pierce me with your blade, Lord Barnard," said Matty, "you who have claimed to love me?"

"I *did* love you!" shouted Lord Barnard. "I wanted to give you all that I have; all I have that is precious and of value would one day have been yours. But you were not satisfied, not grateful for my love and my generosity. No, you took the one thing I could not give you, the one thing both God and the Crown understand is mine. Mine and mine alone!"

Lord Barnard's emphatic rationale bellowed through the open windows and began to attract a small crowd outside the house. Upham and Gallagher were closest to the door; they never continued on to their homes, but waited at a distance until they saw Darnell and Finster enter. Now they were joined by others, and the stirring outside the house was also soon noticed by Alexandra, who was out walking in the hope that the fresh air would clear the nausea and lightheadedness she felt.

"When the sun still shone overhead, you were my son in deed and in fact," Lord Barnard continued. "To kill my own son is a repulsive thought. But no son who lays with his father's wife can go unpunished. And as it is you who have shown hatred and dishonor to me, I will kill you not as my son, but as my enemy."

Suddenly Finster broke in. "Lord Barnard, I must protest. No good can come of this action. Let us retire to discuss a more rational resolution to this unfortunate situation."

"Silence!" ordered Lord Barnard. "As a businessman, I will negotiate many things, but never my honor. I'll hear not a word from you, nor from Darnell. Nor," addressing Lady Barnard for the first time, "from you. Now, Musgrave, raise your sword."

Matty did as he was told. Resigned to a fate he had so long eluded, he thought only briefly of how he would attack. Holding the sword in his right hand, he crossed his arm over his chest and drew the weapon back over his left shoulder, as if to take a backhanded course. He then swiftly circled the sword above his head and came down instead with a forward blow from the right.

Lord Barnard parried the simple attempt at deception, and with a turn of his wrist drew Matty's sword hand back. Matty's front fully exposed and vulnerable, Lord Barnard lunged his right arm forward, his sword plunging into Matty's belly, and the collective gasp and cry of the observers in the room masked the fact that Matty took his wound silently.

Outside the house, Alexandra came upon the small crowd, finding all ears cocked to hear the goings-on within.

"What is the matter?" she asked someone at the rear of the group. "Dunno," came the reply. "Bit of a row going on up the stairs."

Alexandra pushed forward to the front of the throng, and posed the same query to Upham.

"Lord Barnard has challenged Matty to a duel," Upham replied.

"What? Whatever for?" asked Alexandra.

"It's not my place to say, madam," said Upham. "But I'd wager that old Matty's days of wooing in this town are no more."

Alexandra ran up the porch steps and let herself in the front door. The downstairs was entirely dark, the candles having long since extinguished themselves, but at the top of the stairs she could see the backsides of Darnell and Finster outside of Lady Barnard's room. She bounded up the stairs and pushed through the two men, entering the room in time to see Matty slumped to his knees, head bowed, as if offering a prayer to Lord Barnard's sword, dripping red before him.

"Matty!" Alexandra screamed, running to her long-time lover. Lord Barnard held her back with his left arm. In his right, he still held his sword, point facing down, inches from where it had entered Matty. Slowly Matty looked up at Alexandra, mouthed the words, "I'm sorry," and fell forward onto the floor, dead.

Darnell came forward and pulled Alexandra back, away from the violent scene, yet she refused to leave the room where the father of her unborn child lay lifeless. Lady Barnard, now on her knees, blanket fallen and naked to the room and all its inhabitants, also screamed, yet her sorrow was nothing compared to the anger she felt to her husband, who had taken from her the one man who had taught her joy, brought her bliss, and made her feel for once grateful to be a woman.

The screams of the two women brought forth a rush up the stairs of all who had been eavesdropping outside. Finster allowed Upham and Gallagher in, then the three blocked the way of the others, preventing them from fully satisfying their prurient urges.

Oblivious to his growing corps of observers, Lord Barnard grabbed Matty's head by the hair and dragged him over to the edge of Lady Barnard's bed.

"Well, my Lady," he said. "You've had my company for nigh on ten years, and you've had an evening with him. So I ask you now: who do you like the best of us, Matty Musgrave or me?"

With all eyes on Lady Barnard, this mysterious woman of whom little was said, from whom little was seen or heard, about whom little was known, this woman who had earned the sympathy of those who knew and disliked her husband but had never felt loved or understood before this night, spoke up now, loud in volume, clear in conviction, freely from her heart, and with angry resolve in her eyes.

"My husband," she said, "hear this and know it to be true. You have given me comfort but never care, pearls but never pleasure. The one manly thing you've ever done has only extinguished my sole chance for happiness in this life. And now you ask me to choose between you and he? Then here is my choice: I'd rather have a kiss from Matty's cold, dead lips than to spend another day with you or your meaningless finery."

Lord Barnard stood transfixed. Never had he heard Lady Barnard speak with such force of opinion, with such ire, with such disparagement of him. Suddenly, he became aware that her outburst, painful as it was to hear on its own, was heard by several others, his friends, servants, and commoners. His right hand – which had gripped the handle of his sword with such strength for so long that it was sweaty, with blood drawn away from the taught, bent knuckles – had thus far killed two people he had loved. Despite the horrible work it had carried out thus far, his hand could not yet rest.

And so again it was raised, again it thrust forward, again a cry went up in the room. For Lord Barnard's sword again found flesh, this time its point piercing Lady Barnard's heart – Darnell could feel the prick in his own chest – its shaft protruding from the center of her cleavage, one pink breast hanging at either side.

As Lord Barnard withdrew his sword, the force of his action caused Lady Barnard to fall forward, tumbling off the bed, and onto Matty's still body.

"Finster," called Lord Barnard, without looking his way, "I shall need a grave, a large grave, of sufficient size so as to contain both these lovers. But make it deep not wide, and bury my Lady at the top, as she is now, for she was of noble kin."

With that, Lord Barnard tossed his sword on the floor. His right hand at last flexed and relaxed. But Darnell, overcome with shock and grief, suddenly tensed and sprang into action. All but leaping over Alexandra, slumped on the floor before him, Darnell grabbed the sword Matty had used in vain, and swung it madly and clumsily at Lord Barnard, slicing his neck. Lord Barnard reached for his wound and fell backwards. Darnell regained his own balance and stabbed Lord Barnard repeatedly in the abdomen, until Finster and Upham restrained him and removed the weapon from his hand.

Darnell, however, felt himself filled with the strength of ten men, and freed himself from their grip. Standing over his master's lifeless body, quickly draining itself of its blood, his mind now was clear and his voice was firm and strong.

"Finster," he said, "you have papers to the effect that I am Lord Barnard's sole heir, is that not true?"

"It is true," Finster replied, "but it is not valid if you take his life yourself."

"All I've done is stop a madman who had murdered three people in barely an hour's time," said Darnell.

"Surely you've a sufficiently skilled legal mind to clear me of fault and entitle me to my claim. There is no one else alive with as much right to his estate as have I."

"In light of the extraordinary circumstances, Darnell, I'm inclined to agree with you," said Finster, coming to his conclusion while surveying the ghastly scene. "And the sooner we can bring these tragic events to closure, the better for all. I'll take on this case first thing in the morning. But first, we must take these bodies and prepare them for burial."

Gallagher, now the only one blocking the doorway, allowed a few of the gawkers in for the purpose of removing the bodies. Finster directed them to lay the corpses on the cart that once had carried deer from the hunt, and told them to take the path into the woods so they could recover Quentin's body as well. All four victims were to be brought to the mortician, whose studio was located just past the tavern. There, in the morning, Finster would make the necessary legal and burial arrangements.

Orders having been given, and a long night ahead for some, the house soon was emptied of the living and the lifeless alike, leaving Darnell and a still-weeping Alexandra alone. Since Darnell's bold speech, neither had said a word. All they could muster was the strength to embrace, to bind themselves together so as to block out the terrible spectacle of the murderous rampage that had just taken place.

"My dearest Alexandra," said Darnell at last. "A more horrible night is unimaginable. I am fearful of what effects there might be for you in witnessing this carnage."

Alexandra looked up at Darnell, her face contorted with grief, her cheeks slick with sorrow. "I cannot believe Matty is gone. I cannot believe any of it. And yet you, Darnell, you were the only man brave enough to act against Lord Barnard. I'm proud of you. And how awful it must have been for you, for I know that you cared for Lady Barnard as well."

"Hear me, Alexandra," said Darnell. "The only person I care for now – and forever – is you. You and your child. Let him be our child. Marry me, Alexandra. You have no reason to say no. Matty is gone and I am no longer a servant. We'll be wealthy, Alexandra, and we'll have our own servants. Please say yes."

"Oh, Darnell, at such a time as now, how can I say yes with a sure mind and a full heart?" asked Alexandra. "I pray you, ask me again a month's time from now and I promise my answer will be pleasing to you. But I need you to swear something to me. This child I have inside me, you know that it is Matty's child. And whether male or female, this child may look like Matty, make his faces and his gestures. Matty's soul and spirit will live through this child. You must promise me that you will love this child and not hold his patrilineage against him."

"I do swear this, Alexandra," said Darnell, taking her hand and squeezing it firmly. "Though Matty and I were ever at odds, we now shall forever be linked, and it is because of our shared love for you."

Darnell and Alexandra kissed, then turned away from the bloody chaos in the room and went out the door, down the stairs, and then down again to Darnell's basement quarters. Though the images and events of the evening left them restless and anxious, eventually they fell asleep and there spent the night in a silent embrace, all now still and serene, save for the gentle kicking of Alexandra's child in her womb.

Chapter 19

Nearly a fortnight passed before Finster completed the burials and all the legalistic maneuvering required to give Darnell title and deed to the Barnard estate, as well as ownership of all the Barnards' assets. Much was done by Finster as the law required it be done, though wherever subjective interpretations of events could be proffered, discretion most often won out over cold, objective facts. After all, the once-honorable Barnard name already had been besmirched by the bloody affair; it would do no good to further inflame outrage and controversy by making some of the more sordid details a matter of public record.

Finster served not only the rule of the law but also the will of his new clients, Darnell and Alexandra. For example, Lord Barnard's final order, that Matty and Lady Barnard be buried together, was, like his order forbidding his wife to attend church, disobeyed. Darnell and Alexandra both were insistent that they be buried in separate coffins, and that the remains of Lord and Lady Barnard be interred adjacent to each other, while Matty's final resting place be near the pond behind the stable where his presence in life was a familiar one.

Quentin's family, aware of his connection to the woods at the edge of which he died, buried him beneath a mammoth oak near the stream.

Darnell and Alexandra also both agreed that they desired not to be master and mistress to a house full of servants. However, given the emotional turmoil they had recently endured and the challenges that lay ahead with Alexandra's pregnancy and Lord Barnard's business affairs, having a cook and a housecleaner would be a great help. And so Finster was asked to rehire those that Lord Barnard had earlier dismissed. The cleaner would handle Alexandra's former laundry chores, enabling her to rest and to get strong and healthy again.

No replacement for Matty as caretaker of the horses was hired. As neither Darnell nor Alexandra were riders, there was no need to keep all four beasts. One was given to Reverend Collins for his personal and pastoral use, and one was given to Quentin's family as compensation for their loss. The remaining two were used to start a private coach business located off the property. Darnell hired Francis Richardson, younger brother of Thomas the tavern keeper, as the driver and manager. Darnell and Alexandra would have use of the coach for their travel needs, and when they did not require the service it would be hired out to others.

Finster completed the business arrangements, including overseeing the construction of a new stable and office just beyond the church.

For Darnell's part, though he was legally Lord Barnard's heir, he sought to distance himself from his former master. He rejected the notion he'd been adopted by him and refused to take his last name. He would take the man's house and his money, yes, but would not adopt for himself Lord Barnard's cruelty and paranoia. Darnell had earned newfound respect from the citizenry and vowed never to be aloof around them or to place himself and his priorities above theirs if he could help it. He never did return to the tavern, however, which suited Alexandra well.

As she had requested, a month after the horror Darnell proposed again to her and this time she accepted. Yet not without conditions. First, Alexandra insisted he reiterate his pledge to be loving to her child, to raise the child as his own, and to never speak ill of Matty. She also strongly encouraged him to remove the shackles of his former position and the comportment it required, and to be more carefree and passionate. She was genuinely impressed with his bold actions that night in Lady Barnard's room, yet that was not the type of passion she desired of him. Alexandra neither expected nor wished for Darnell to become like Matty; she only wanted him to enjoy his days – and if he could, she would help him to enjoy his nights as well.

As for Lady Barnard's room, the site of three bloody murders, it was thoroughly cleaned, from the floor and the walls to the linens and the furniture. Then Alexandra asked that the doors be bolted shut, that no one should ever again enter or use the room, and so not to have the awful memory of that night relived each time one made use of it.

At first, Darnell was reluctant to comply, for there were valuable items in her room and it had always exuded a warm, appealing femininity so lacking in the rest of the house. Yet he acceded, for he knew well that he could not be sure of his own ability to remain stoic in that space, given his prior history there in Lady Barnard's presence, and the carnage he witnessed and contributed to only a month before.

As summer dawned, Darnell and Alexandra were married in a small, private ceremony performed by Reverend Collins. Only Finster and Alexandra's cousin Andrew attended. With the warmer weather, Alexandra donned lighter dress and her state was just beginning to become apparent to observers. She had long recognized that she stood to be an object of scorn among the villagers; indeed, she knew there were whispers about her from those aware of her liaisons with Matty – in particular from those who knew that Matty favored her among all his other conquests, for if she was most favored she must also be most experienced.

Yet Darnell was uncomfortable, self-conscious even, about the gossip. On his many trips into town on behalf of either Lord or Lady Barnard, he'd learned to keep a sharp ear tuned to rumors, never once betraying by his expression that he was eavesdropping on those who always regarded his presence in town with curiosity. For after all, only he knew the truth behind their suppositions, and what a blessing and a curse it had been to hold such intimate knowledge about such an enigmatic couple.

Now, with Alexandra clearly pregnant longer than married, he was sensitive to chatter, and he confided as such to her one night.

"Alexandra, I am deeply concerned with what I hear in town about your…your status," he said.

"Ah, pay them no mind, dear one," she replied. "If they've nothing better to occupy their minds with, that says more about their status than it does mine."

"Nevertheless, I hear it in town and it makes me angry," he said. "It makes me want to confront them, but I don't, and then I feel I am failing to uphold your honor. I just think it would be better for us – for all of us, the baby as well – if we lived elsewhere."

"Lived elsewhere? What do you mean? Are you suggesting we leave here, our home for so many years, a home we now own rather than work in, simply because of idle gossip?"

"I'm not suggesting it, Alexandra," Darnell backpedaled. "I've just been…thinking…that it would be a good thing for us to start over. In a new county, perhaps."

Alexandra stared at him, trying not to show anger. She knew his intentions were good. Yet she also wondered and worried about whether Darnell had yet attained the strength and resilience she hoped he was accruing in the days and weeks since he so boldly and instinctively wielded Lord Barnard's sword. Further, she had heard Darnell, no longer held by the duty and discretion of his former position, tell her of Lord Barnard's maniacal obsession with what the villagers thought of him. Could Darnell be adopting such an attitude as well?

Finally, she spoke, in soft, measured tone, with her hands upon her husband's arms.

"I am sorry, Darnell, that you are hurt by what others may be saying about me. But please let me assure you that I am not bothered by it. And surely they will soon find something else to talk about. I want to stay here. My cousin is here, and he is the only family I know anymore." *And I cannot leave Matty's grave*, she kept to herself.

"I am not deaf to your wishes, my darling," said Darnell, "yet all I desire for us is a fresh start, a new beginning, as we prepare to welcome our child into our lives." *And in leaving we would not have Matty's grave so close by to serve as a constant reminder*, he added in thought.

"Darnell, every day we are making a new life for ourselves," she replied. "This is all new to us. We are new together. Newly married, learning our way around each other. Soon to be parents for the first time, not knowing what to do. Our home is the one familiar thing we possess, the one source of stability we have. We must cling to it, not desert it. If we leave our home, we will be as autumn leaves in the wind. I won't have it," she insisted. "I'm sorry, Darnell, but I won't."

And with that, he relented.

To help Darnell face his fears and increase his comfort in their new life and their current home, Alexandra insisted nightly that they walk into the village, visit the shops, be as visible, social, and unselfconscious as possible. In time, the citizens came to view them not as former servants but as masters of their own lives, not as undeserving lowlifes who fell into fortune but as kind, pleasant, and polite people who were generous with their time and friendship. Her plan worked, and Darnell – though still immutably aloof and unnecessarily formal – indeed became more comfortable and never again raised the notion of leaving Lancashire.

Summer passed, its heat carried off by the cooler breezes of autumn, which rustled the fiery leaves of orange and gold and broke them from the trees. The more agreeable weather suited Alexandra, easing the growing burden she carried in her abdomen. Thus she retained her energy and vigor through the middle of November before the imminence of her baby's birth finally forced her to rest and await the pains that would bring the child into the world.

Ultimately, it was another fortnight before the baby began to wend its way from its warm, secure home inside Alexandra's body to the cold, uncertain space of Lady Barnard's room. Yes, Alexandra had lately changed her mind about keeping its door bolted shut, believing that by doing so she was preserving it unchanged as a room of death. By giving birth in that room, she would restore it to one of life. And the baby's first breath would take place mere inches from where its father took his last.

So it was that in the early hours of December, with encouragement and guidance from the village midwife, and Darnell pacing the floor downstairs, that Alexandra gave birth to a son. Healthy and well-formed, the boy's robust cry brought Darnell bounding up the stairs and into the room. As he held his son, Darnell looked at the face and saw reflected back the dark hair and eyes of the father, and the sweet nose and lips of the mother. He was instantly smitten.

Alexandra wanted to name him Matthew but out of respect for Darnell's feelings she instead suggested Henry, for no other reason than she liked the name. Darnell, his heart open, his dream fulfilled, his life now triumphant with a beautiful wife, a darling child, a stately home, and wealth enough to ensure the long-term comfort of all, agreed.

"Welcome, Henry," he said. "Know that you are loved. From love were you made, in love shall you be raised."

Alexandra smiled. She was content. Henry cried. He was hungry. Outside, a light snow, really just a frozen mist, began to fall. The cold of winter was returning, and yet the sun was rising, casting an orange glow on the pond behind the empty stable, on the stone marker on Matty's nearby grave, and on the once-unhappy house that now was a loving home to three people at peace, together in embrace on a bed with the languid hues of light through colored glass gently creeping over them.

* * *